THAT HAIR

Djaimilia Pereira de Almeida

translated by Eric M. B. Becker

 TIN HOUSE BOOKS / Portland, Oregon

Published by Tin House Books, Portland, Oregon

Distributed by W. W. Norton & Company

Library of Congress Cataloging-in-Publication Data
Names: Almeida, Djaimilia Pereira de, 1982- author. | Becker, Eric M. B.,
    translator.
Title: That hair / Djaimilia Pereira de Almeida ; translated by Eric M.B.
    Becker.
Other titles: Esse cabelo. English
Description: Portland, Oregon : Tin House Books, [2020] | Translated from
    Portuguese into English.
Identifiers: LCCN 2019042836 | ISBN 9781947793415 (paperback) | ISBN
    9781947793507 (ebook)
Subjects: LCSH: Almeida, Djaimilia Pereira de, 1982---Fiction. | GSAFD:
    Autobiographical fiction.
Classification: LCC PQ9929.A456 E8613 2020 | DDC 869.3/5--dc23
LC record available at https://lccn.loc.gov/2019042836

First US Edition 2020
Printed in the USA
Interior design by Diane Chonette
www.tinhouse.com

For Humberto

Giving thanks for having a country of one's own is like being grateful for having an arm. How would I write if I were to lose this arm? Writing with a pencil between the teeth is a way of standing on ceremony with ourselves. Witnesses swear to me that I am the most Portuguese of all the Portuguese members of my family. It's as if they were always greeting me with an "Ah, France! Anatole, Anatole!" the way Lévi-Strauss was greeted in a village in the Brazilian countryside. The only family members we manage to speak with, however, are those who are unable to respond. We operate under the belief that this family interprets the world for us when in reality we spend our lives translating the new world into their language. I say to Lévi-Strauss: "This is my aunt, she's a great admirer of yours." Lévi-Strauss invariably replies: "Ah, France! Anatole . . . ," etc. To write with a pencil between one's teeth is to write to a villager who finds himself before his first Frenchman. The matter of knowing who is responding to what we write might provide us with relief from our miniature interests, bringing us to imagine that what we say is important, despite it all. To stand on ceremony with what it is we have to say is, however, a form of blindness. Writing has little to do with imagination and resembles a way of coming to deserve the lack of a response. Our life is overrun all the time by this taciturn family—memory—the way Thatcher feared that English culture would be overrun by immigrants.

Translator's Note by Eric M. B. Becker

EXPEDITIONS INTO THE DEPTHS OF IDENTITY

In 2017, a couple of months after I'd first translated work by Djaimilia Pereira de Almeida, I found myself in the middle of a brief stopover in Lisbon on my way to a literary festival in Cabo Verde; some Brazilian friends had sent me their own personal guide (a sentimental one, perhaps?) to the city. They recommended I trace a path from the traditionally bohemian Chiado—home to the iconic Fernando Pessoa statue—to the Feira da Ladra, a 900-year-old market in the Graça neighborhood. Along the steep and winding ascent to Graça, I passed the sun-bleached façade of the Igreja de São Vicente de Fora. Its edifice dates back to the time of Afonso I—the first king to rule Portugal following the expulsion of the Moors in 1147—and the church serves as the burial site for many of the members of the Brigantine Dynasty. (Its art collection features an eighteenth-century ivory statue of Jesus from Goa, a Portuguese colony until 1961.) The whole structure might be seen as an emblem of the nation, from the siege of Lisbon in the middle of the twelfth century through the end of Portugal's colonial project in the late twentieth.

My intention that Tuesday afternoon was to visit the used book stands, a Lisboeta version, perhaps, of Paris's Left Bank bouquinistes or the ever rarer sight of used book dealers lining the sidewalks of New York's Upper West Side. I came away with a few volumes that are now within comfortable reach of my desk in New York, but it was an encounter with a man selling antique stamps that had the greatest impact on me. A congenial man initially, he quickly pivoted to his time in the Portuguese army during the 1960s and '70s, when several of the country's African colonies waged wars for independence. My interlocutor wasn't, he explained earnestly, opposed to their sovereignty, but he was deeply offended by the way the Portuguese "handed everything over on a silver platter" to their former subjects.

It is in this context, barely forty years removed from the independence of Angola, that Djaimilia Pereira de Almeida's *That Hair* steps in to plumb the depths of Portugal's grisly history—its broader consequences, but above all its personal costs. Like her narrator, Mila, Almeida was born to a family that is Portuguese on one side and Angolan on the other. Like her narrator—"the most Portuguese of all the Portuguese members of my family"—Almeida moved from Luanda to Lisbon at a young age and is at once entirely Angolan and entirely Lisboeta. However, Mila's indomitable hair is a constant reminder that she doesn't entirely belong in Portugal, while her childhood exploits with her cousins in the streets of Lisbon are proof that the city is not entirely *not* hers, either.

"The truth is that the story of my curly hair intersects with the story of at least two countries and, by extension, the underlying story of the relations among several continents: a geopolitics," Almeida writes in the opening pages of this hybrid novel, which sits somewhere between fiction and the essay (another genre at which she excels).

The story of the four-year-old Angolan girl who would grow up Portuguese traverses not only landscapes—from the Rossio to Mozambique to Little Rock, Arkansas—but eras. Photo albums from Mila's Lisbon childhood in the 1980s and '90s, and old films from her Portuguese family's African days, amount to more than a personal story—concomitantly, they form a story of colonialism, of enduring racial and gender prejudices, of reparations.

If the thematic material of *That Hair* is vast, so too is the gamut of other literary works with which it dialogues. Within Portuguese-language literature of the postcolonial era (which includes writers such as António Lobo Antunes), or from the perspective of those Portuguese who returned following the African colonies' wars of liberation (such as Lídia Jorge), or the work of African writers like José Eduardo Agualusa or Mia Couto, Almeida's is a first: the first work to be written from the perspective of one who left Africa for Lisbon, and whose family history straddles both the Iberian Peninsula and Portuguese Africa.

It would, however, be folly to read Almeida's work in a Lusophone context alone. *That Hair* is also of a piece with Nigerian novelist Chimamanda Ngozi Adichie's *Americanah*, English writer Zadie Smith's *Swing Time*, or Somali Italian writer Igiaba Scego's *Adua*. Like these writers, Almeida is concerned with exploring the spaces between cultures, the vagaries of identity and belonging.

Almeida's sources also stretch back much further than the recent past. In *That Hair*, Mila's search for her origins is a search à la Whitman for the multitudes within, as the author herself has acknowledged. The reference to Whitman necessarily recalls Pessoa. Other influences include Benjamin's *Berlin Childhood around 1900*, with its "expeditions into the depths of memory," and Danielle Allen's writing on Will Counts's iconic 1957 photo of Elizabeth Eckford on her way to integrate Central High School in Little Rock. ("It is the portrait of a self-persecution and the daily struggle to achieve indifference," Mila posits during her own reckoning with this "X-ray of my soul.")

Translating an X-ray of the soul is no ordinary task. Portuguese and English are, often, languages at odds with each other. Whereas much of mainstream writing in English since the time of Hemingway has favored the short sentence, Portuguese is many times more permissive of and malleable to discursive detours, repeated pivots, and elliptical flights of lyrical fancy, all in the same phrase. A challenge I faced from the outset, with this book and every book I've translated, was deciding what was simply Portuguese and what was a matter of style. There's a philosophical bent to Almeida's work, which, as Portuguese critic Isabel Lucas described it, operates as extended soliloquy. In a book riddled with questions and few straight answers, it was clear that the digressions, the sentences that sometimes stretched a page and beyond, were Almeida's way of including the reader in Mila's arduous journey toward self-discovery, of fostering understanding and common cause.

The expedition into, or excavation of, memory that is central to *That Hair* unfolds in the context of Mila's confessed unease at writing the biography of her hair ("How might I write this story so as to avoid the trap of intolerable frivolity?"). It's a discomfort that recalls Virginia Woolf's reservations about the biography (or "life-writing") and its related genres, from her weariness of "the damned egotistical self" to misgivings about "[writing] directly about the soul. Looked at, it vanishes" (*Virginia Woolf*, by Hermione Lee). Almeida, through Mila, takes that position one step further, claiming: "Memory is a demagogue: it doesn't allow us to choose what we see; it thrives on the temptation to make less of the people we *were not*." At every turn in this journey to the past, there is the risk of reinforcing caricature where one seeks an origin. There is always "the trap of sentimentality" to be avoided.

It would be wrong to situate Almeida within this pantheon and risk leaving her novel desiccated, by which I mean that I want to properly appreciate the vitality and urgency of her narrative on its own terms. *That Hair* is not only an exploration of identity, race, and a stagnant past; it is one possible manifestation of American intellectual Christina Sharpe's concept of "wake work," a process of recognizing the legacy of colonialism and its racist systems that thrive to the present day. Sharpe's multitudinal metaphor of the wake—as keeping watch with the dead, the path left by a ship, the consequences of a racist past that stretches across borders and seas, and, finally, as an awakening to consciousness—is the heartbeat of *That Hair* (a work that preceded Sharpe's *In the Wake: On Blackness and Being* by just one year). It is present in the rejection Mila faces at certain Lisbon salons, in her sojourns to far-flung hair studios, in her remote journey toward the ruins of the past. Writes Almeida, "It is we who . . . survive as if the only castle in a miles-wide radius: a sign that life once existed where today there's only dead grass, olive trees, and cork oaks."

As Mila exhumes and interrogates these signs of life, she soon finds that her true discoveries are made along the way, via detours, in the places and artifacts that lie beyond what was sought. She finds questions of nationalism, of who is permitted to belong and what that belonging means, and of the borders—real and imaginary—that exercise so much more influence over some lives than others. In *That Hair*, the question Almeida seems to be asking of all of us is: If we are so often the details we considered mere incidentals in our search for ourselves, who then are the people we claim to be?

June 2019
New York, NY

THAT HAIR

1

My mother cut my hair for the first time when I was six months old. The hair, which according to several witnesses and a few photographs had been soft and straight, was reborn coiled and dry. I don't know if this sums up my still-short life. One could quite easily say just the opposite. To this day, along the curve of my nape, the hair still grows inexplicably straight, the soft hair of a newborn, which I treat as a vestige. The story of my hair begins with this first haircut. How might I write this story so as to avoid the trap of intolerable frivolity? No one would accuse the biography of an arm of being frivolous; and yet it's impossible to tell the story of its fleeting movements—mechanical, irretrievable, lost to oblivion. Perhaps this might sound insensitive to veterans of war or amputees, whose imaginations conjure pains they can still feel, rounds of applause, runs along the beach. It wouldn't do me much good, I imagine, to fantasize over the reconquest of my head by the soft-stranded survivors near the curve of my neck. The truth is that the story of my curly hair intersects with the story of at least two countries and, by extension, the underlying story of the relations among several continents: a geopolitics.

Perhaps the place to begin this biography of my hair is many decades ago, in Luanda, with a girl named Constança, a coy blonde (a fetching "typist girl," perhaps?), the unspoken youthful passion of my black grandfather, Castro Pinto, long before he became head nurse at Luanda's Hospital Maria Pia; or perhaps I ought to begin with the night I surprised him with braids that he found divine. I'd spent nine hours sitting cross-legged on the floor at the hairdresser, head between the legs of two particularly ruthless young girls, who in the midst of doing my hair interrupted their task to turn some feijoada and rice pudding from lunch into a bean soup, and I felt a warm sensation on my back (and a vague odor) coming from between their legs. "What a sight!" he said. Indeed: perhaps the story of my hair has its origin in this girl Constança, whom I'm not related to in any way, but whose presence my grandfather seemed to seek in my relaxed hair and in the girls on the bus that, after he was already an old man living on the outskirts of Lisbon, would take him each morning to his job at Cimov where, his back hunched, he swept the floors until the day he died. How to tell this history with sobriety and the desired discretion?

Perhaps someone has already written a book about hair, problem solved, but no one's written the story of *my* hair, as I was painfully reminded by two fake blondes to whom I once temporarily surrendered my curls for a hopeless "brushing"—two women who, no less ruthless than the others, pulled my hair this way and that and commented aloud, "It's full of split ends," as they waged battle against their own arms (the masculinity of which, with their swollen biceps bulging from beneath their smocks, provided me, the entire time, with a secret form of revenge for the torture they inflicted). The haunted house that every hair salon represents for the young woman I've become is often all I have left of my connection to Africa and the history of the dignity of my ancestors. However, I do have plenty of suffering and corrective brushings after returning home from the "beauty parlor," as my mother calls it, and plenty of attempts not to take too personally the work of these hairdressers whose implacability and incompetence I never summoned the courage to confront. The story I can tell is a catalog of salons, with Portugal's corresponding history of ethnic transformations—from the fifty-year-old returnees to the Moldavian manicurists forced to adopt

Brazilian methods—undergoing countless treatments to tame the natural exuberance of a young lady who, in the words of these same women, was a "good girl." The story of surrendering my education in what it meant to be a woman to the public sphere is not, perhaps, the fairy tale of miscegenation, but rather a story of reparations.

No white woman on a city bus ever gave my Grandpa Castro the time of day. Humming Bakongo canticles to himself, Papá was a man whom you would never suspect of carrying this time-honored tradition with him as he sat next to you on the bus. A man of invisible traditions—and what a ring this would have to it, capitalized: The Man of Invisible Traditions, a true original. No one ever looked at him, this man who, by his own account, was rather cranky, "the Portuguese kid," as he was known as a young man, who was always shouting, "Put it in the goal, you monkey," referring to black soccer players, and who categorized people according to their resemblance to certain jungle animals, even describing himself as "the monkey *type*," the kind of person who patiently waits for the conversation to come to a close before proffering his wisdom.

I come from generations of lunatics, which is perhaps a sign that what takes place inside the heads of my ancestors is more important than what goes on around them. The family to whom I owe my hair have described the journey between Portugal and Angola in ships and airplanes over four generations with the nonchalance of those accustomed to travel. A nonchalance that nonetheless was not passed on to me and throws into stark relief my own dread of travel; a dread of each trip that—out of an instinct to cling to life that never assails me on solid ground—I constantly fear will be my last. Legend has it I stepped off the plane in Portugal at the age of three clinging to a package of Maria crackers, my hair in a particularly rebellious state. I came dressed in a yellow wool camisole that can still be seen today in an old passport photo notable for my wide smile, the product of a felicitous misunderstanding about the significance of being photographed. I'm laughing with joy, or perhaps incited for some comic motive by one of my adult family members, whom I reencounter tanned and sporting beards in photographs of the newborn me splayed atop the bedsheets.

And meanwhile it's my hair—not the mental abyss—that day in and day out brings me back to this story. For as long as I can remember, I've woken up with a rebellious mane, so often at odds with my journey, no sign of the headscarves recommended for covering one's hair while sleeping. To say that I wake up with a lion's mane out of carelessness is to say that I wake up every day with at least a modicum of embarrassment or a motive to laugh at myself in the mirror: a motive accompanied by impatience and, at times, rage. It's occurred to me that I might owe the daily reminder of what ties me to my family to the haircut I received at six months of age. I've been told I'm a *mulata das pedras*, as they say in Angola, not the idealized beauty that *mulata* conjures for them but a second-rate one, and with bad hair to boot. This expression always blinds me with the memory of rocks along the beach: slippery, slimy stones difficult to navigate with bare feet.

The lunacy of my ancestors factors into the story of my hair like anything else that demands silence; it is a condition from which the hair might be an ennobling escape, a victory of aesthetics over life, as though hair were either a question of life or aesthetics, but never both. At the same time, my deceased ancestors rise up around me. As I speak they return as versions of themselves distinct from the way I remember them. This is not the story of their states of mind, which I would never dare to tell, but that of the meeting between grace and circumstance, the encounter of the book with its hair. There is nothing to say of hair that does not pose a problem. To say something consists of bringing to the surface that which, because it is second nature, often remains undetected.

Stepping off the plane, evoking the image of a statesman's lover who lands hours after the plane full of government officials, the girlish Constança would begin by unbuttoning her jacket. The steamy Luanda air hinted at the long-awaited absence of her aunts from strolls through the park, during which, by simple miracle, there's nothing to suggest that she'd been discovered walking hand in hand with my grandfather. From the state of the weather to the state of the state, she traded bits of conversation in exchange for being hand-fed biscuits dipped in tea. I can identify in her Papá's noble carriage, in the era's high-waisted pants, the coat, the hat, a certain uprightness that his old immigrant's hunchback would later subdue. During the newscast's commercial break—a toothpaste ad—Constança was a frequent subject of conversation between my grandfather and me, our fear of hurting my grandmother's feelings often interrupting. But it was also a pretext to blackmail an irritated Grandpa Castro: either he gave us money for candy or "Hey, what about that blonde girl?"—as though we'd divined that there was more to this girl than the promise of fresh breath and reduced tartar. I leave her here, like a half-empty tube of Couto-brand toothpaste, abandoned in a plastic cup covered in a layer of mineral scum, next to the toothbrushes, in memory of my dear Grandma Maria, in whom a burning jealousy took root that would last for the rest of her life.

I never did take the bus route with Papá to Cimov, a place that comes back to me now in almost mythic proportions. I don't know what the city would look like if I were to see it with his eyes. Today, I find myself thinking of the row of high-rises along the way—a steely gray against the darkness—like an image of my grandfather's thoughts, of his introspective manner as he sat on the bus in those pre-dawn hours. It was always quite clear to him what the day would hold. A wandering repairman of household goods, he always had a passion for widgets: first, gauze, syringes, scalpels; later, first aid kits, pain-relief balms, razor blades wrapped in paper, Bactrim, thermoses, plastic bags, pens, the pocket of his shirt misshapen by blocks of lottery tickets and folded sheets of paper where he had worked out the algorithm for what, according to him, were the winning numbers.

There's nothing romantic about these things. The pain-relief balm and the rusty medical supplies were simply instruments from life as a nurse in Luanda, which he saw no reason to forget and which he in fact never left behind. He maintained the very same routine, diligently applied to his kin, of injections, medical prescriptions, and a few home circumcisions, which by a stroke of luck all the boys survived. The minute anyone sneezed or complained of a migraine, he would administer antibiotics; and he contin-ued doing so, deaf to our protests, for the rest of his days.

He'd attended nursing school in Angola, studying by candlelight, a habit he would pay for with a premature case of cataracts. He prided himself on having survived the entire course on only bananas and peanuts, a diet he recounted to me sometime during the '90s, already in this other hemisphere, with the same nostalgia with which he used to speak of the butter and marmalade of our family's golden years. Ever since I was a little girl, I've pictured him studying, half-naked in his hut, the lantern tucked beneath his chin, angled toward his books—as though, in an implausible synthesis of times and places, he were a greenhorn working on the railroad, fearing a coyote attack on his camp as he slept—battling insomnia, the heat, mosquitoes; but I know all too well that nothing could be further from the truth. In Papá's house in Luanda, where I would spend school vacations, everyone still ate margarine from a giant can, something I'd never seen before. As they scraped pans clean in the afternoon heat, the neighbor girls listened to my stories of Portugal. I introduced them to the concept of an "escalator," which caused them to break out in song: "I'm happy as can be, there's nothing else I want for me." Not so many years later, as Papá left the house at sunrise, off to the bus and to Cimov, the air on the outskirts of Lisbon—laden with the refreshing chill of morning dew that I too would come to love—saturated everything with the vague scent of ammonia.

In the early morning hours when my Grandpa Castro was born, his father was at sea. This in M'Banza Kongo, in Angola's Zaire province, a place that has assumed mythic status in the family lore. In the distance, on the beach, the albino man's blond hair was a speck of light on the horizon. He could often be found fishing with spear amid the rocks, waiting until a fish appeared. The next moment, the fish would burst out of the water, dark blood spurting everywhere, bringing into focus the fisherman's own reflection against the surface. At times, on similar mornings when the tide was full at the break of day, the man would raise his spear into the air, parting the sea and taking his time as he crossed the gap, strolling between the parted waters, the waves forming a soaring wall at his side. He would never do this in the company of others or in a moment of danger, only when enjoying a stroll alone. However, being the only one to attest to a gift he could not share with others left him convinced he was one of the chosen. The satisfaction gained appears to have had an inverse relationship to the size of his audience: it was a ceremony to be performed in solitude. The day my Grandpa Castro was born, his father had left the house with a certain fish in mind, something special he'd seen swimming nearby. The beach was empty, the fog hovered low. As if he found himself before the only fish alive, my great-grandfather steadied himself on a rock, ready to pounce, stretching his arm skyward and holding his silhouette pose—milk on oil—his hair behind him in one long tress, as the fish darted below and then burst to the surface with all its size and weight. At home, his wife gave birth to a son. As the fisherman had foreseen, and as others later confirmed, the little Castro child had spoken, not cried, as he emerged into the dark of the ramshackle hut illuminated with fish-oil lamps, reeking of fish as all such huts did. It's possible there aren't even beaches or fish in M'Banza Kongo.

I inherited from my Grandpa Castro a collection of imitation Parker pens he had stored inside a suitcase for the previous decade. He had come to Portugal in 1984 with the aim of seeking treatment at a hospital in Lisbon for one of his sons, who had been born with one leg shorter than the other. The leg required medical treatment unavailable in Angola at that time. He came to Portugal not as an immigrant in search of work, but as a father, staying longer than expected and then remaining, to the tune of operations and physical therapy, until the end of his life, a pleasant coda to Angolan years. In Lisbon, he and his son found lodging in boardinghouses near the hospital, as a great number of Portuguese Africa's ill did at the time and still do, whether for the duration of their medical treatments or indefinitely.

At the entrance to the Pensão Covilhã, kitty-corner from the Casa de Amigos in Paredes de Coura, the ill take in the Lisbon air. One of them has a bandage over one eye, another a gangrenous thigh, an arm protected by a tattooed cast that's begun to crumble, a chopstick re-purposed to itch beneath the layers of plaster and cotton. They are the remnants of empire, accidental Camões at the tender age of nine, spared from becoming childhood mortality statistics so that they might enjoy what to them seems like a vacation in the city. Even with a bit of luck, they are destined, each and every one, to discover in Portugal nothing more than the world from which they've come.

Visiting the Covilhã is like sticking one's nose into an old suitcase. The boardinghouse doesn't carry the scent of alcohol one smells in hospitals, but that of ointments past their expiration dates mixed with the rotting odor of infections and a faint metallic note like blood, traces of mothballs, a concoction at once chemical and organic, attenuated by the tang of ketchup or Old Spice spilling from upended bottles into the suitcase between strands of hair and iodine tincture, rendering a package of Valium useless. My grandfather, dozing off to this odor with a perfect forbearance, asks my uncle if the room doesn't smell of woman. "It's just your imagination—go to sleep, Papá," his boy responds.

In the tavern next door, the sick make conversation with old men in whom, despite some initial repugnance, they inspire a measure of compassion. The sick take the day's sports section from one of the tables back to their rooms at the Covilhã and celebrate each Belenenses goal scored the Sunday prior. The sight of the ill provokes strong reactions in the old men, sometimes ruining their appetites before they've even left home or inducing vomiting, transporting them back to the war and to their youth; but they stifle such anguish and downplay it to their wives, telling them that a deviled egg didn't sit quite right or that "Tio Zeca must be serving bad wine, the sneaky bastard." These same men frequently offer a deviled egg to their young friends, something the younger group has never seen, or introduce them to the ketchup they then proceed to get all over their noses as they eat. "Go on, squirt, make a wish!" they goad the kids, explaining that's how it's done when you try something for the very first time, an explanation that doesn't quite compute.

And that's how, between stepping on dog shit in open-toe sandals (which they sport in spite of the autumn weather) and making love to *placards* advertising Olá-brand ice cream—reason in itself to live—the sick young men spend their days trying out new flavors and the old men redeem themselves for the queasy sensation they experience at the sight of the young men, a queasiness they dismiss with a wave: "OK, OK, OK." Then the little squirts close their eyes and ask for a Perna de Pau. It's in this exchange that the old men reveal themselves to be good souls, though they have only themselves in mind throughout this entire marathon, patiently awaiting the kids' reactions in order that they might feel something for the young people before their eyes.

Lisbon's teeming Covilhã is not some charming countryside inn but a roadside leper colony, simultaneously at the very center of the city and at the margins, because it only takes one wrong turn for you to find yourself in the middle of nowhere. From their bedrooms, the sick can see between the window bars to the back of the hospital; they watch as the trash is collected and entertain the hope of a larger room, envisioned just beyond the gray walls of a building that more closely resembles a factory than a health-care facility.

Often, the sick spend years at the Covilhã. They manage only a glimpse of the city, and of the country nothing beyond the concept of *chanfana*, which Dona Olga—a woman who probably comes from Seia and is owner of the boardinghouse—translates for them on good days, when she isn't busy calling everything a pigsty as soon as she's had a glance at the mountains of suitcases, dirty clothes, and empty bottles that characterize the rooms of the sick, rooms she never enters and from which can be heard the sound of a cassette tape playing the *lambada*. The sense of Portugal one gathers from the lobby of the Pensão Covilhã is that of the country's typical dishes, the basis of our ignorance about any country: a banquet of rudimentary explanations, about the taste of pork rinds, the taste of snow peas, the taste of pig's blood stew. The garden must be ripe for the picking this time of year, think Dona Olga and the legion of the sick.

My grandfather stashed the pens he would later bequeath to me in one of his suitcases over a period of ten years, rusty utensils wound together with a piece of string.

He had come prepared to assume obligations, provide signatures, sign contracts, when what really awaited him was years of sharing a bathroom, years his aftershave went unused. A decade later, he would leave the Covilhã for São Gens, a shantytown on the outskirts of Lisbon, sending for his wife and other children in Angola, storing the very same half-unpacked suitcases beneath a new bed, in a new house filled with the same whiff of old suitcase.

2

The very first salon I ever went to was tucked alongside a steep street in Sapadores that I would come upon again by chance when moving neighborhoods some twenty years later. We walked quite some distance, my mother and I; she was taking her summer vacations in Oeiras, staying with my Grandma Lúcia and Grandpa Manuel (on my father's side), in whose house I grew up. This time, however, we didn't walk so much as we had on a previous expedition to nearby Barreiro. I retain the memory of an interminable wait—an allegory for my life—for the ferry we referred to as "the boat to Cacilhas," rather imprecisely. Though we hadn't boarded at the Cais do Sodré or gone to the beach but rather to get my hair done on the other side of the Tagus, this trip to Barreiro leaps from the pages of Ramalho Ortigão's guide to the river's beaches. I can picture my mother there, out of place, unnerved by the twentieth century, by the public transport system whose existence has made this story of African hair salons possible. "There are species of fish who care for their offspring," Ramalho writes, in an apt description of my mother and me: trout who bury their eggs in secluded coves. We'd missed the last boat: that's the only possible explanation. We'd missed the last boat and spent the night at the wharf, gas lamps casting their glow upon us, and in the cold, ruining our hair as we rested our heads against a wooden bench. (Or was it all a dream?)

To this day, when I think back to Sapadores, I'm flooded with the dizzying scent of ammonia and the memory of walking down some stairs to a cramped basement with white walls, a salon whose excessive zeal for cleanliness, common among the poor, denoted luxury to my six-year-old eyes. There's little I remember beyond the hot-pink packaging of a hair relaxer called Soft & Free (or was it Dark & Lovely?), whose children's variety featured smiling black children with straight hair, instant role models. False advertising, I would realize the next day. The treatment (whose abrasive chemicals require the use of latex gloves) consisted of "opening up the hair," leaving it more supple, they explained to me. (This trip to Sapadores had, in reality, been preceded by a memorable test-run closer to home with Dona Esperança, my

Grandma Lúcia's hairdresser. Unwilling to accept the
state of my hair, she grabbed a dryer and a brush and,
during the brief interludes between fixing my grandmother's hair, generously straightened out two tufts of
hair to prove it wasn't a lost cause. "You see? Didn't I
tell you that Mila has beautiful hair? It's only a question
of straightening it out a bit and—voilà!" We left Dona
Esperança's holding hands: my grandmother with her
typical perm, me with my tufts of hair stretched until
they hung over my ears, which we didn't touch so we
could show them off at home, the two of us attempt-
ing to hide our doubts about this miraculous fix. My
grandfather expressed his approval with his eyebrows,
giving us to understand that this "women's business" was
neither his concern nor within his sphere of interest,
placing responsibility for an unlikely solution—this, also,
done with his eyebrows—squarely in my grandmother's
hands.) Opening up the hair was, in fact, something else
entirely. I would be lying if I said I remember the ritual
visited upon my head in Sapadores, but it's unlikely to
have included anything out of the ordinary. First, they
must have sat me on a chair with a pillow beneath my
rear, and I must have undone my slapdash hairdo. In the
mirror, I could see behind my back to the salon, where
there may have been other people getting their hair done,
too. Someone would have then parted my hair into four
sections, brushing much too hard with a fine-tooth comb.

Later, someone else would have forgotten to protect my scalp with the recommended cream, a precaution often dispensed with by those who've undergone this experience with some frequency. I also cannot remember how I left Sapadores. This baptism was, then, also my rebirth: to the horrifying thought that the hairdressers had forgotten about me after the waiting time necessary for the product to take effect, and to the impression that they were speaking behind my back, wicked tongues. At that moment, I was reborn with a high degree of paranoia about my hair and, at the same time, with a certain idea of what a woman should be. On the packages of hair relaxer, there was a girl who, my mother contended, was not black, sporting a polka-dot jumpsuit, the first outfit I can remember: a brand-new jumpsuit that I would one day wear to a birthday party. Hours before the party, the jumpsuit got a stain, which I fixed by cutting it out with scissors; which I then fixed by cutting away a bit more, until there was a gigantic hole in the jumpsuit—which, in the end, I may never have actually used. This was the first in a series of techniques I would develop to conceal clothing stains, such as sewing buttons over each splotch.

The "good girl" had learned to sew buttons with Dona Antónia, my Grandma Lúcia's seamstress, who would visit once a week to spend the afternoon at the same desk where I learned to write, darning socks and mending seams, glasses resting on the tip of her pointy little nose. Dona

Antónia, whose anachronistic head—an impeccable perm on a black head of hair—I never gave a moment's peace, was not as dear to me as Dona Lurdes, whose unmemorable head of hair visited us each and every day. I never lacked for conversation with Dona Lurdes, who would leave a trace of sodium hydroxide when she left and whose house I once visited. She lived in São Domingos de Rana. As she worked, the three of us would talk in the kitchen: me, her, and Grandma Lúcia—a fact that exasperated my Grandpa Manuel, who would then summon me and my grandma to the living room, complaining, "Don't stay there talking all alone, you two." On such afternoons, I learned from Dona Lurdes the art of talking without saying a thing, a social skill my Grandpa Castro abhorred, but which I consider a practical skill of great moral utility. I asked after her children—who were growing up in São Domingos de Rana and every now and then would visit us, blushing with shyness—as though I weren't also growing up there in the kitchen, and I spoke to her about the goings-on at school, same as always. In my role as cute kid at a retirement home—building things with matchsticks on the living room floor, later moving on to sewing, confusing *elbows* with *shoulders* or *heels* day after day as though to mark the passage of time, triggering lessons that lasted entire afternoons, or pooping on the carpet merely to be able to examine the result closely—I had no idea what it meant for my grandparents to be "retired."

Given the way we all faced the unique patterns of our own deformations and the moment in which we then found ourselves, today I think that we must have approached my acts of mischief and their corresponding censure as though they were nothing more than growing pains. In fact, it is the ignorance of having crossed through certain stages of our journey, epitomized in my encounter with Grandma Lúcia and Grandpa Manuel, arbitrary in a cosmic sense yet full of purpose, which made this encounter between people something beyond a mere family relationship. "We're all so old now," sighed my grandmother at the end of her life, generalizing. Lúcia freed herself of her ignorance the day she realized we were all adults. The aging of those around her, then, had the power of a revelation, be it of her own past, be it that she belonged to a particular species, as though we were the final generation and nothing would come after us.

It would be two decades before I would visit Sapadores again. Long before my move from one neighborhood to another, and for many years indeed, the area was nothing more than a distant memory, a place I forgot about for long periods of time. "Sapadores" was nothing more than a stop I sometimes crossed while riding the bus, as obscure to me as "Senhor Roubado" or "Poço do Bispo," places I would go to braid my hair, a necessity that carried with it the virtue of expanding my knowledge of Lisbon. Whether I've actually taken one of these bus lines, I cannot say, since—without any way to distinguish the truth from mere impressions—I could not swear that all my childhood trips to hairdressers haven't caused me to imagine setting foot in these places. Sometimes, when I've taken a wrong turn, I have a case of déjà vu, the sensation of walking through a new place with the feeling that I've been there before. I note, however, with surprise, that the exact same thing could be said of my memories of Angola.

At this point, I've managed to keep intact a mental image of the Hotel Turismo with its bullet-ridden pockmarks, this still in the '90s; the Teatro Avenida; the entryway of the *Jornal de Angola*, the noxious paint fumes, streets that I could not possibly know my way around. Today, when I see Luanda on TV, its skyline cluttered with cranes, there's not much more I'm able to recognize. Of all the rest, I retain only the same idea I have of Sapadores, an idea that comes back to us when we pass through a place we've been before. It's as though Luanda were merely on the other side of Odivelas, another stop along a nearby bus route, just tricky to reach. In a balancing act between memory and the moment, I realize that my reconstruction of Luanda proceeds hand in hand with my own reconstruction. On tree trunks and the doors of public restrooms, scrawled letters read: "X was here." What, I ask myself, could this inscription be referring to?

This is a story of short-lived solutions: hairdos that were impossible to maintain and that proved a disappointment the very next day, if not sooner. Through the years, I have learned a great deal about routines and maintenance techniques; every so often during a conversation, I come across a new morning ritual for stretching out my hair or a recommendation to moisturize it every week with a mask. I have not, however, experienced any of this, only the moments preceding each trip to the hairdresser, which are like a labored uphill climb followed by a hairpin curve: then, the precipice. All my hairdos—each of which is, I admit, nothing more than this—have lasted for only the brief instant before I step out into the humid street, where they are soon disfigured; or before I lay my head down on a pillow, tossing and turning on any given night, in a struggle against my very nature. I give in to frivolity, you could say. As time has passed, my scruple with regard to frivolity has given way to the realization that this very scruple is frivolous, as though the moral of a story could be rooted in letting it be what it is, and not in what it says.

Center stage in a family photo taken in the early '90s, alongside all manner of bangs, bowl cuts, grunge-dos, and a series of unnameable triangular disasters (two sad, straight tufts of hair combed off to the side and topped by a pseudo-ponytail discolored by the sun), are the hairdos of my Portuguese family members. Marking the point at which I stopped counting, the photograph shows that we were sixteen cousins in all, a number that, despite the fact that there were really nineteen of us, became fixed in my mind, the same way that, for years, my mind never moved on from the time my father was thirty-six years old, or the year I was nine (as I was on the day the portrait was taken), as though my entire childhood lasted a single year. In the photograph, we're standing next to one another behind a sofa, at the home of my Grandma Lúcia and Grandpa Manuel. Behind us is the wall hanging that, at the time, I considered the very definition of good taste.

As it would be for any nine-year-old girl, combing my Grandma Lúcia's hair (I lived with her at the time) was one of my favorite pastimes. Her hair exuded the perfume of a bygone era, a scent I've never again come across: the scent of Feno de Portugal soap, tobacco, and oiliness, which I came to love. Later I would find, scattered throughout the house and several drawers, photographs of my grandmother as a young woman, her hair a shimmering black, flawlessly arranged as she stood on a veranda in Beira, or, in a slide my grandfather projected on the wall, waving amid pigeons in the wind by the side of a fountain in Italy. Grandma's black hair had been lost along the way or, it seemed to me then, had been reborn on the heads of a few cousins of mine, where, though they were still girls, it was reborn strong and determined: a woman's hair, a legacy whose elegance still awaited them, disguised in the family photo beneath hideous, comical bangs that covered the girls' eyes. Of those heirs to my grandmother's hair, not a single one suspected at the time the blessing that had been bestowed on them: a vibrant, spectacular inheritance. I would discreetly stick my nose into Grandma Lúcia's hair, being careful not to become distracted and brush too hard (or else "playtime's over"). This scent was the first place where I suspected I had an origin, long before the images of rocks on the beach entered my mind, a projection resulting from a cruel metaphor. I often think about how this scent is all that I have to say about my identity. A cousin who is visiting makes the comment that I'm "miles away from being a real Angolan." He's right. To my great chagrin, it's not acceptable to tell the border patrol that my country of origin is my grandmother's hair. And yet knowing where I'm from would seem crucial to telling the story of my hair, a never-ending act of remembering not windy street corners in Oeiras around the year 1990, not rocks or certain scents, but a concrete origin, an origin in the most common meaning of the word.

I'm surprised by the overlap between who I am and the narrative of my origins. Only by embracing the irrelevance of each hairdo, every one a diversionary crown, can I take a step back. The fact that it takes a hefty wind to upset my hair is something of an irony. It has survived

all sorts of disturbances, like a plant whose soil outlives
the shattering of a vase. Doing justice to these senso-
rial forms of origin could by chance save me from the
misfortune of thinking of myself within the confines of
a stereotype. Would an authentic cosmopolitanism be
that much more preferable to the parochial scent of an
old lady, vestige of the intersecting lives of a wandering salesman from Portugal making his way through
the Congo, an albino fisherman from M'Banza Kongo,
Catholic elders from Seia, New Christian Masons from
Castelo Branco, my ancestors? Perhaps the one advan-
tage of my confessed ignorance as to the topography of
Luanda is to protect me from a stream of Lusophone
commonplaces, replaced by still others to which I'm not
always sensitive, and which I guard against like a pot-
bellied night watchman. The most obvious and literary
commonplace, that of seeing in my hair a reflection of
the mind, is the reason behind this Story of My Hair,
which up until now I never had much time for. A story
that nonetheless is the result of distraction, as though
for years I had forgotten the experience under way on
the top of my head, with a negligence that, in retrospect,
seems methodical, so that one day I might have something to talk about. Grandma Lúcia exuded the scent of
the place I come from, my homeland, the scent of stale
air, of a retired person, of artificial light.

Grandma Lúcia's father, a Portuguese man who went around selling knickknacks by traveling caravan in what is today Kinshasa, set off for Africa as a newlywed at the dawn of the twentieth century. His wife, a woman of fragile health, gave birth to little Lúcia and two more siblings, only to succumb to tuberculosis a few years later. Lúcia's father would then send his children to Seia, his deceased wife's hometown, to be raised by two of her cousins. The children grew up under the cousins' care as though they'd been born there. And yet they were from Congo, which no one would ever have guessed from their starched bibs. One of the children became bishop. The other two, my Grandma Lúcia and her sister, became schoolteachers. Of the caravan selling fabrics, soap, burlap sacks, and cookware, there was but silence for many years. Manuel, whom Lúcia would marry at the age of nineteen, often disregarded his family's salesman past, though he was proud at the thought of having an African wife, a fact that lent him a certain aura of a man of the world, much to his liking. It was for this reason that he would speak to her quite naturally of leaving for Africa as an engineer, at the invitation of a hydroelectric company, to construct dams. One of the consequences of colonization at that time was the widespread notion that those Africans like my Grandma Lúcia never actually returned to the land of their birth simply by boarding a ship. Lúcia was returning to where she came from, despite the feeling that she was leaving home—she immigrated to the place where she had come into the world: a sort of migration within the self. My grandparents would arrive in Beira, in Mozambique, after marrying in Seia one damp morning.

For four decades, my great-grandfather the salesman was a ghost from whom no one heard a thing. Perhaps at some point, off wherever he was, somewhere on the margins of a tributary of the Congo River, he had opened a lodge or killed some black man in a brawl. One day, when Grandma Lúcia and Grandpa Manuel arrived in Luanda, years after disembarking in Mozambique, where the bulk of their children were born, a man knocked on their door. My grandparents took him in, caring for him until his death with a diligence they hadn't shown when it came to preserving his memory. He had returned there to die, having somehow located his daughter. I have no way of knowing if he felt as if he'd returned to the caravan, as if to a place he'd buried treasure. Maybe my grandmother had mourned her absent father, had mourned her young mother throughout her years in Africa and throughout her years in Portugal. They were part of her, like an elastic band around her wrist meant to remind her of something she'd unwittingly thrown away before its time, forgetting what had brought her there in the first place, the way she did when I was a little girl and her memory failed her. No one in the family inherited the sagacity of the caravan man, though all have found it necessary to defy the uprooting of his young wife.

In her retirement, Grandma Lúcia would make some tea for her sister, Justina, who lived in Porto at the time and would come to visit every now and then. In the living room of the apartment in Oeiras, Aunt Justina marveled at the knitting that kept my grandmother busy during that period. They would discuss everything from the atmospheric pressure in the Azores or the construction of another highway to a lovers' spat over politics. From the living room, against the background of arbitrariness that brought them together, two women could be seen at work on a flower bed, delivering themselves entirely to the inconsequence they attributed to one another's opinions ("Have you seen Vacondeus?") and revealing to me, as I watched their encounter unfold, the way in which courtesy is the attentive channeling of disinterest—which there's nothing wrong with, of course.

If Aunt Justina felt like it, the visit would be celebrated with a pound cake she had made, saturated with the same fragrance I had smelled on her neck when I greeted her upon arrival—the fragrance, I bet, of the drawers of her house. And so tea was accompanied by cake, amid sighs directed at the dessert's timeless, unchanging flavor: few things alleviated the burden of sisterhood like a candied cherry. Chewing its dry, tasteless flesh relieved them for a few moments of the obligation to make conversation. They were two horses with the same owner, stall-mates in the same stable, little more than any other two souls brought together by chance.

A scourge of palm weevils, *Rhynchophorus ferrugineus*, had eaten away at the palm trees along Cesário Verde Promenade, where I would stroll with my Grandma Lúcia in that era. The weevils had flown in from Polynesia and East Asia to southern Europe, devastating palm trees from the Algarve to Lisbon. I ask myself how long their journey must have been. On my way home, I'm greeted by six ominous tree stumps. What can be said amounts to what can be said given that remembering anything beyond who I am is not a possibility. I'm not open to remembering anything beyond who I am. We need the help of the outer world to remind us of one another. The scene before me became a map of this need. Palm tree stumps are, in spite of this, a perfectly sufficient yield for posterity. It's these amputated stumps that will greet us in the future and that now, after I've finally dared to probe deeper, give me the impression of having brought the era of my hair to an end. Calendars and ecology, obsolete. The eras follow one right after another, according to the mysterious rules that govern the life cycles of animals we often ignore. City employees close off large areas so as not to harm pedestrians or property while they see to the trees; wearing yellow helmets, they climb a revolving ladder; they butcher the palm trees with electric saws; they prune the canopies of others, revealing the true height of their trunks. By the hand of biblical set designers, the metaphors of my book have become literal. Succumbing to the baldness to which the city council, like some overzealous Delilah, has condemned them, these specters no longer weigh over my story. The age of Oeiras has come to an end.

Escalators were a novelty when, at the age of eight, I became confidante to a woman who sold chandeliers and crystal at Centro Comercial Europa, just beneath the apartment where we lived. In the store, in a rotating display against which, completely mesmerized, I scrunched my nose, I stood in awe of a fairy tale in which crystal owls, butterflies, and beetles acquired bluish and lilac physiques as the sun crept through the shop window, which faced the street. Behind the shop window, which led to a smoke shop, an escalator flowed, which I stood admiring from afar.

While all this passed through my mind, the woman from the store complained about her husband, as though no one could hear her. At the time, I didn't know it was already possible to glimpse my future as an archivist. The absolute stillness of the crystal pieces corresponded to an exchange between expectation and disappointment, suspension and promise. Exactly like a museum visitor standing before a painting, lingering before a work that has stunned her with her own likeness, removing her glasses to get a better look, apprehensively reaching for the canvas, reading the caption, before continuing as though it were nothing. During a break in the woman's litany of complaints, I would run over to the escalator where I would linger, watching customers ride up and down. Then, like a fly, I'd leap to another spot, another bit of conversation. "Where did you run off to?" the saleswoman would ask me. "Careful on the escalator!" The warning went in one ear and out the other, the way I cycled through one store, then another, another saleswoman, another perfume sample. Lévi-Strauss tells the story of a Native American man who ended up as a doorman at the University of California. Before that, and for quite some time, he had wandered the streets, lost and hungry, without anyone noticing he was there. It's more or less the same way with memory, were he not a faithful reflection of my own jaunts through Centro Comercial Europa in the late 1980s—the refined version of the teatime ritual I witnessed, wild hair in a yellow jumpsuit, during those same years—quietly listening to the adults one minute, the next absorbed in daydreams that are as unintelligible to me today as they would be for a stranger. Before this act of remembering became document and rumination, these afternoons without a country—spent entertaining or tormenting saleswomen, or longing after a cake with the adulterated smell of perfume (and despite the fact that the countdown toward our common extinction was already in motion)—were the Native American's urban crucible. This is the tranquil coda to all that, pairing names to faces in a retrospective roll call.

3

Our love of the superfluous is helpful in better understanding ourselves. I return to a familiar spot, the little
house with its zinc roofing on the outskirts of Lisbon
that belonged to my maternal grandparents, to see once
again the only flower I've ever come across in São Gens:
an artificial flower ravaged by the sun. Below a certain
threshold of privilege, there may not be a place for such
passionate dedication to things otherwise expendable.
Satisfy our basic conditions of survival, however, and our
total commitment to the superfluous is what defines our
humanity. The artificial rose whisks me back to a past far
removed from my fascination for the unruly green verandas of Lisbon, each summoning me as I make my way
through the city. With plants like that, a madwoman

must live there, I think as I gaze at the chaotic gardens. The spectacle of madness displayed on these verandas is a privilege conferred by their owners' status as citizens. A privilege of my own citizenship is my trifling fascination for such manifestations of madness and the disinterest of the other passersby. It's as if only in our own country are we permitted to put our madness on parade without regard to the others around us, only in our own country do we have such a luxury.

My Angolan grandfather's dashed dream of becoming a Portuguese citizen coincides with the artificial rose a neighbor lady once offered to my Grandma Maria. This rose was a sign, however indirect, that there was no room for the superfluous in Castro Pinto's life, unlike the madwomen who turned over their verandas to their plants, since without them they found it impossible to live. Madness and full citizenship are linked, then, in a most unexpected way. The fear that a country's culture might succumb to immigrant hands was, in all its folly, reflected in the way my Grandpa Castro sung elegiac Bakong spirituals to himself on the bus that took him to Cimov each day, fearing the curiosity of his fellow riders, that they might think he was talking to himself, mistaking him for a madman. (When I asked him why he sang, he told me he was greeting death.) Fear of being mistaken for a madman is in any event a sign of not feeling at home. I take for mad these accidental gardeners of Lisbon's verandas, but I could simply take them for Portuguese, suspended there on the edifices in the form of parasites. The disregard I always paid my hair comes back to me as a sign that here I feel at home, just as my Angolan family in São Gens had said I would. I speak of this hair, but, without any loss of meaning or precision, I could well speak of this head.

My Grandpa Castro—a *kimpovela* (as if I knew how to write in Kikongo), having spoken rather than cried at birth, a man who one day would creep up on his father as the older man raised his lance and parted the sea in a village where there's no sea to speak of—had no time for plants, though a decade of toil at Cimov had transformed his body through constant exercise, covering him in a cloak, slowly turning him into its bitter contents. Beneath his worn shirt and pants, he could well have been returning by bus from the cotton fields, my grandfather, lean and muscular, his abdomen unexpectedly chiseled. Having left at five in the morning, it would be eight at night by the time he returned to São Gens, loaded down by a cooler full of leftovers from the Cimov canteen: roasted potatoes and some stale bread. With the hands of a gardener and his nails trimmed by razor blade, my Grandpa Castro would wash my Grandma Maria's hair, its long and silver strands, years on end, always leaving behind some shampoo that the low water pressure was no help in removing.

She would let forth cries of pain and pleasure, she'd say "Papá, gentle," as though they were making love, while the rest of us cackled in the other room just two steps away. All this happened one August in the '90s, in São Gens, my summer vacation. There were times, I think now, when no one would have heard them, no one would have been at home to laugh. And then they were just two old people in a slow and dangerous drama (she ran the risk of falling each time she took a bath, falling in the bath, falling as she got out of the bath), a showerhead without enough pressure for so much hair, a considerable inconvenience. Maria found joy in these baths all the same, in the energetic scrubbing of her body—clothes in a washtub, and not a person who was only half-alive. At times, a mirthful laugh escaped. When my grandparents on both sides were still alive, I always thought of them as two happy couples.

My white grandmother (how might I say that without it sounding like a Brazilian soap opera?) was always asking about my hair: "Tell me, Mila, when are you going to take care of *that hair*?" In those years, my hair was its own persona, an alter ego there in the room. My Angolan grandmother was a black Fula woman named Maria da Luz. (Did I already mention this?) Nana, who when still a youth became chairbound thanks to a blood clot, spent her twilight years sitting at a table, or at a window, admiring the distant mountainside that separated her from

Amadora (it might as well have been Moscow), accompanying the life cycle of rabbits in a rabbit pen in her front yard whose only true residents were two old rags, making conversation with the neighbor ladies who hung the clothes out to dry with the help of lengthy wooden poles, and who was—how could she hide it?—an invalid whose story you could tell based on the places she never set foot, the Lisbon that she would never come to know, the bus that she would never take, the color of streets she never strolled, never diverting her gaze from the omnipresent Elephant Man—this same Maria da Luz swelled with pride at my hair. The Lisbon she knew was hearsay, but Lisbon is also this harmless gossip. My grandmother's story could be the monotonous biography of an arm, a leg, which I came to know as scaly, leaden limbs.

In the summer, I'd set out early with some cousins from São Gens to run wild in the streets of Lisbon, the whole gang donning unisex tracksuits, oversize hooded sweatshirts purchased in the Praça de Espanha; we'd hit the track, listening to the Wu-Tang Clan on our Discmans, without the least idea what the lyrics were saying and imagining that the warning found on the CD cover, "Parental Advisory: Explicit Content," meant that they were genuine, *real*. "Watch ya step, kid," they warned, "protect ya neck." I'm not being shameless when I bring up the sights my grandmother never saw: the touristic and incomplete itinerary that, for us, was Lisbon. I don't believe Nana ever once saw a single pigeon in Rossio, or a single one of its madmen, the Tagus, the bridge, the Chiado, the Centro Colombo. Today, I think that Maria da Luz would have seen the charm in the way the clothes drying on the line danced in the wind. For her, Portugal was these clothes dancing in the wind. By the age of twelve, my cousins and I were no longer free to live in this ignorance.

The truncated city we roved traced the contours of our inner life, whose tacit course followed the shadowy gaps between subway stations, where a silent truce imposed itself among us kids, or was interrupted when the Cypress Hill album playing on our Discmans skipped each time we quickened our steps. What would be the private consequences of our amputated sense of Lisbon, of the hopes we carried in tow through the work sites along Restauradores and Colégio Militar, detours in traffic routes and on sidewalks, around exposed pipes beneath wooden slabs, around boards through whose gaps we would sneak up on construction workers, our compatriots, having lunch or washing up, of the prospect of new music megastores, as though we were flocking there to buy coffee and gloves, admire cats in the windows, drink cherry liqueur, pose with Pessoa, and not only, to the exclusion of all other aims, to lift our spirits. What if the lives of the Lisboetas were closed off to us, as ours were to them, and it was they instead who were invisible?

We waited for the construction to end without the least bit of impatience, and, after some time, it would indeed have been strange if it had ever ended, and the new metro, the new terminal, the new *shopping* had made the leap from promise to concrete reality, marking the dawn of a new age. Perhaps this sketch is not entirely reliable, and perhaps during those years the Baixa was not in fact a dejected construction site. Whatever the case, for us, the only thing that would last in the end was these sites. Me and my cousins, the prehistory of all the intimidation, the life of our curiosity, our common perception of never being old enough—all that's left of these things is the never-ending work at Restauradores, which required the relocation of Bimotor, a tiny music store adjacent to the Gelataria Veneziana, to a glass structure a few feet ahead, which we took such a liking to that, construction at an end, we considered the original the simulacrum.

I don't regret that traversing this itinerary of attractions may have left us with an incomplete idea of ourselves, or that Nana never came to know Lisbon in any depth. It would have been more just had Maria da Luz been the one to dirty her shoes with the dust on Restauradores, if she had stood in wonder before the site where the Colombo was being erected, if at the end of our outing she had gotten a McDonald's sundae all over her face; if Maria had lived within us, a flea in our pocket as we crossed the Baixa. This meant, however, that it fell to Castro Pinto, and not the children of the house, to help Maria get around. She was the reason for his early mornings blanketed in fog, the unnamed addressee of the goodbye letter that was those years in Europe: years spent atop the hunch in his spine, in the rough hands that washed her hair, on the walk to the bus stop, which her dead leg kept her from without hope of remedy, transforming Papá's body into the host of Maria's twilight years. It was not in some far-flung post, in some paradise to which life in Portugal had come to lead them, that their common salvation resided, but in my grandmother's lifeless leg, her entire European old age a redemptive impediment. Maria da Luz's life would not be salvaged by a common, respectable existence in Portugal, but in allowing her a look into our Lisbon, where no one realized that we were all on our own, a place so clearly reflected in what memory of her remains: a construction site that was nothing more than a *reminder of life*, as Nietzsche wrote of his father.

Watching television one afternoon, we caught a performance by a folk music group on a program broadcast live from a small town in the countryside. As they sang, I instinctively swayed with the rhythm to Grandma Maria's horror. "Look at you wagging your tail with the likes of them!" a cousin of mine cried and pointed at me, the clumsy Kizomba apprentice. He spent the entire summer calling me "my little Portuguese," prompting me to turn bright red. The affectionate epithet was testament to the erroneous belief that Portugal is a place where everyone listens and dances to folk music. The caricatured notion of nationality that made it to São Gens via the television—and was countered by the course of a domestic life that, in its crudeness, made a mockery of the very ideas of caricature and nationality—later led me to the realization, in hindsight, of the gap between who we were and what was stereotype. To say that we owe our idiosyncrasies to the quill of a colonial writer would be the equivalent of casting a cynical gaze upon a moving excursion of almond-flower devotees simply because these trees flower each year. An admonishment for these faithful excursionists, returning each year to bear witness once again to the peculiarity of each almond tree, each spring, each excursion. The way others at home treated my hair was always symbolic of the confusion between affection and prejudice, and this has always been an excuse for my own shortcomings in caring for it. People at home would say I treat it the way a little Portuguese or a woman miles away from being a real Angolan would. And yet I live out my yearning for São Gens as a yearning not for the person I could never have been but for a caricature.

I ask myself what Grandma Maria would discuss with the neighbor women at the window, what they might have had to talk about. What would she think of the world seen via the television, a stream of light? How presumptuous of me to say such a thing, I think, expecting cause to feel shame. A person needs almost nothing to maintain her inner flame, a motive for joy. Life before Grandma Maria's fall seems to have been plenty for the lessons she would later impart to me, as though she were then at her zenith following a prefatory period during which she managed to get out and about on her own, and not the other way around.

In Oeiras, before the salons, the buses, and the "boat to Cacilhas," I was taken to see a certain Dona Mena on the third floor, an older woman of mixed heritage who cut hair out of her home, but I no longer retain any images from this time, except for a makeshift sink in the bathroom and a foot dryer in another room, the first in a long, nightmarish cycle of waiting for my hair, wound up in rollers, to take form as it dried. I arrived home with a ponytail. My photo was taken for a new green passport, where I appear with a giant gap between my front teeth. I have no memory of my mane the next day, but I no doubt exhibited it with pride. I would see Dona Mena quite frequently in the elevator: she would ask about my hair and offer advice, an external reminder of my own disillusionment. That's how life is when we're children: an enjambment of vaccines, diaper changes, ever-changing laps, haircuts, hands to take our hands as we cross the street, stimuli to which we respond first by screaming and later become accustomed. The shared custody of my hair expresses a human condition that our adult tantrums seek to disguise. Perhaps I ought to say that's how it is *since* the time we're children, as life often seems like a never-ending interregnum of passivity, during which we become our own people. Ointment for a chapped little bottom, advice against the suitability of new bangs or the shaving of some family member's mustache, a bath to combat lice—perhaps these are our grown-up dramas, administered by others in an alliance of solidarity to which our assent is the only correct response.

The ponytail would fall down the same abyss where all my hairstyles fell and from which I am still capable of salvaging a ritual I would dedicate myself to over some months, years later, in which I would sleep with my hair in rollers as I waited for it to dry overnight, without any way of resting my head on the pillow. These were months of torment, filled with frequent dreams of Jesus, to whom I would appeal before falling asleep, rereading—in the New World Translation of the Holy Scriptures my Grandma Maria would use during Bible study with the Jehovah's Witnesses—the verses of the most recent homily, which it had fallen to me to summarize for my Grandma Lúcia. In the morning, in front of the mirror, I would brush my still-damp curls, as though it were some game, until the effect of the curlers was negated by the attempt to craft them into a hairstyle.

Here I am before the mirror by morning, when all my efforts are cast aside and I'm taken back to a sweeter time, prior to the advance of my aesthetic frustrations into a disgust that lasts the entire day, like a moral failing, a curse. A time when botching our hair is still a trivial detail, when we have yet to play for keeps or master the art of feeling our stomachs turn at our appearance. It is the briefest of amnesties—sweet, sure, but ever so empty—so brief that we cannot even nurture the hope of cherishing its memory. This frustration with my hair remained with me as it mutated from a scarcely noticeable itch into an abrasive rash: the mutation of aesthetics into morality, of hair dryer into judge, of clumsiness into fatalism, of aborted hairstyle into guilt, damnation—of the ruthless hairdresser into psychosis. Making peace with ourselves is, I think to myself, like making peace with our ancestry, as though being at ease in our own skin were the consequence of the comfort brought by having a family. This is where the forces split—render unto aesthetics what belongs to aesthetics, to morality what belongs to morality—until, at the very next instant, we find ourselves facing the impossibility that such a separation of forces could ever take place. Realizing that we've become a shambles of beauty and virtue, that to expurgate it, something we are unable to do, would be to empty it of meaning—that it's not only the winsome and remote amnesty from poorly executed childhood haircuts that is fleeting, but that this transience also defines the interval during which we imagine ourselves capable of the alchemy required to decant the elements of this mixture we have become. One day, I may even learn to tame my hair. I cannot, however, do so in another person's skin.

The furniture at the house in São Gens came from the brothers of the local congregation of Jehovah's Witnesses, whose service Grandma Maria drove to once a week, her only outing, and the time when, during the ride and in the minutes it took the brothers to put her into the car and help her back out, she glimpsed through the car window what she would come to know of the surrounding neighborhoods. The brothers wore suits on their way to bear witness, walking side by side down the street as if they weren't about to try to approach anyone, or stopping at a street corner, at a park bench, where they would loft hopeful catcalls to passersby, waving them over with an illustrated pamphlet notable for the bunches of bananas and pineapples that leapt forth from its cover.

It was these same brothers who would bring my grandmother a measure of relief, filling her idle hours, paying her a visit, recounting an episode from other people's lives, bringing her a tiny vase that was just right for an artificial rose, repairing her television, all with an unabated selflessness. They would emerge from a car wearing sunglasses as they sought to conceal their inherent mechanics' air, their fingernails, dirtied at the shop, washed for service but still blackened, men seeking within themselves the manners of their clients, if just for a day. As I summon them forth here, they bring me back to the Moldavian man who for years I would see at a certain café in the evenings, dressed in a suit as he drank a glass of whiskey clutched in a hand filthy with paint. They led a double life, is what I mean to say, my Grandma Maria's guardian angels, in their quiet rendition in which I had detected fanaticism, complete conviction that they would be among the chosen, without ever stopping to ask, "But why me, if we are so many?" It was an existence for which they found their reward on Sundays in the Kingdom Hall: a pavilion where everyone sat in beach chairs. Perhaps this was their benediction, that of being saved from skepticism. They would extend a slice of pineapple to me, these men for whom each street corner held the latent possibility of salvation, treating me like a relation separated from the flock, missing one of its teeth. To my surprise, I would find them in São Gens doing my grandmother's nails at the living room table while she nibbled on sweet rolls that her "manicurist" had snuck for her; or me looking for a flea in the mattress in the back of the dark bedroom, on the bed where Maria slept, beneath which—as though the many years had not intervened and because there was no other space—she kept her luggage from the trip from Luanda, her baptism by flight. Irreplaceable, they would say to her, "Aren't you a sight, all happy with your little grand-daughter. She looks just like her grandma."

4

Back when I still considered my hair to be a trivial matter, we lived in fear of a pack of bullies who went about stealing backpacks, watches, and tennis shoes from children as they left school. The year was 1992. The leader of the pack, a street kid who had got a girl pregnant prematurely, was known as the Raven. One day he was even interviewed by the neighborhood newspaper. We all quaked at the thought of this Raven, as though he lay in wait above the schoolyard pavilions to grab us along the short trajectory to the bus that would take us home. At that age, I didn't know whether it was any safer to run to the bus, replete with its own ne'er-do-wells and a crazed driver who sped along at a hundred an hour, the bus nearly overturning at roundabouts, or whether to continue home on foot via a tunnel where some graffiti urged me to destroy the waves and not the beaches. The Raven sees us even if we cannot see him, I would think to myself. Now and then, tears were shed over yet another Monte Campo backpack or pair of Redley tennis shoes. On the worst days, some unfortunate ten-year-old was sent home without his clothes. In between classes, the kids ran behind the school buildings, yelling, "The Raven's over there!" I never saw anyone, all the same.

There was no Raven, I think today. There were no schoolyard robberies or vandalized bus stops, broken windows; there was not even a pregnant girl. Before me, old family photographs I scour in search of meanings, connections, an explanation for it all. Sometimes, the explanations we seek are a pack of bullies we've never seen. There is no explanation, though we speak of nothing else.

I arrived in Portugal in '85, from Angola. My father had gone ahead of me a year earlier, returning to take a new job. It was toward the end of the '70s in Luanda, when he was barely past twenty, that he'd met my mother. When I am the last remaining witness, and I can no longer remember whether it was at the post office, the consulate, the television station, or at the beach that my parents met, my grandchildren will console themselves with the half-written book that is as much as I do know, and as much as they'll ever know, about my parents' courtship and eventual marriage. When I can no longer remember if my mother wore her hair down or in a beaded toque, if hers was a chapel or a sweep train, if everything took place in private, if at the customshouse or on the beach; when the only thing left from the past is that train, how beautiful such and such neighbor looked, the potency of this or that seasoning, the yellowish tone of a balustrade, the way everything smelled of paint, my grandchildren will say, "Again, Grandma," and suddenly the yellow will become musty, I'll add *jindungo* to the seasoning, I'll embellish the neighbor woman with a hat, in an effort to keep myself from disappearing, to avoid being swallowed up. "Your grandfather had a moped that looked like a wildebeest and terrorized Luanda from end to end," I'll tell them. This will be as much as made it to my ears, related in the belief that our years of courtship and youth could withstand time only in the form of myth. I picture my father's moped circling around a Luanda that is the ornament of my forebears' extinction. It symbolizes the itinerary I've invented for these years: grilled fish and boiled cassava on Sundays in Grandpa Castro's house; a house in the neighborhood of Prenda; another in Kinaxixi: my mother's accent, "black made white," as they said back then; neighbor women of whom the only remaining memory will be their uncommon beauty. "She was so beautiful, that girl, the city stretched on forever, how that wildebeest purred." I follow the trail left by the motor scooter through the streets, knowing even before I begin that we know one other via telegram. "Unlike so many Portuguese, your great-grandparents didn't return to Portugal in the '70s." I often sensed in my Grandpa Manuel a certain ambivalence toward those who returned. He would tell me that he had nothing to run from, he was at home. He later returned with my Grandma Lúcia in the early '80s, after they'd retired, taking Portugal as their retirement retreat. It's staggering to think that I only ever knew them in their retirement, that they simply did not exist in my life while still of working age.

One day I will be a great-grandmother. I will live and breathe my great-grandchildren's swimming lessons, chlorine, awkward dives, their first strokes, following in the footsteps of Castro Pinto, of Manuel, of Lúcia, of Maria da Luz. The footsteps of little Tico, my beloved great-grandson, of little Lisa, our baby, on whose hair I'll enact not frustrated dreams but frustrated haircuts long past the time my hands allow it.

One day, this book will sustain me the way it would someone shown an old photo album and told that she was even pretty, just like the Jehovah's Witnesses used to tell my Grandma Maria da Luz when she needed consoling. Perhaps then it will be clear to me the way all of childhood is a childhood album—when the day arrives that this book is my oxygen and I can no longer remember what I've recounted in its pages, and memory's mawkishness is surpassed by the mawkishness of the end. Then I'll succumb to my own vanity, turning the pages, a vanity that marks the end of being an individual, while all around us someone scurries to bring a glass of water to our mouths, a damp towel, a straw, a thermometer, among empty perfume bottles, shadows, the stench, and remote controls; meanwhile, a birthday celebration, and my conscience whispers that's enough, come on now, *time to go home.*

Grandma Lúcia and Grandpa Manuel moved from Beira to Luanda in early 1970, taking with them their children who weren't yet on their own. My father crisscrossed the city on his moped, sometimes carrying a crate full of beers, which scattered along the way to the joy of passersby. "Wasn't it a raven?" Tico asks me. "Again, Grandma." Let these be the last words I hear.

5

The period during which I didn't give much thought to my hair lasted fourteen years. Up until then, nature had given me hair that shot out every which way. I would tame it with barrettes, or else I'd wear my hair short, a cut just like my mother wore for many years. You shape short hair, she explained to me, by covering a wet head with a towel and batting the hair in little circles until it becomes "nice and round." On weekends, when I was a child, my father, cousins, a school friend, and I would grab the streetcar to the Cais do Sodré to spend the day in Lisbon, or we would pack lunch boxes for picnics in Carcavelos or the Estádio do Jamor, outings that always ended with us wearing masks made of forest grasses, easy to stick into my dry hair. I had the perfect hair for Carnaval, a source of pride.

That was the time of *Tieta*, the Brazilian soap opera I followed with my back turned to the television, for months stifling the instinct to laugh on account of a dirty word in the theme song. That song would provide me with my first experience with exegesis, centered on the line "*Tieta do Agreste* / The moon full of lust," which could only mean "moon full of willies," my cousins and I concluded, though such a thing seemed unintelligible to us. Why would the moon be full of little willies, I asked myself, and who was putting them there?

We caught wind of the possibilities in the German photonovels a neighbor had at home and that always ended with the young girls about to faint, lying on their backs and covered in milk. "But why *milk*?" a neighbor girl asked me. "Can't you see they look hungry?" came my ready response. That must have been it, we agreed, curiosity sated, and we ran outside to play doctors and nurses, subjecting the youngest to the wrath of our authority, rubbing our bodies against the others and planting kisses on the cousins just like in *Tieta*. The older kids listened to a Nirvana cassette tape with a floating baby on the cover. One song talked about a mulatto and a mosquito, words I felt a certain affinity with but whose connection to my life escapes me even today. Perhaps it was about Luanda, or malaria.

At school, a myth was circulating at the time involving girls who'd lost their virginity while exercising or riding a bike, breaking the hymen. In a diary from this time, protected by a minuscule gold lock, I wrote one day that I thought I'd lost my virginity. ("I think I fucked.") The diary fell into the hands of my uncle, who showed it to my grandmother. I had convinced myself that I'd made love with a younger cousin, adding to my tally of sins at the dinner table, horrified at the thought of my grandmother broaching the subject. The problem wasn't the transgression, news of which she received as naturally as someone adding a flower to a bouquet—it was the prospect of someone mentioning the curse word used in the diary at the table. In the end, my private confession amounted to this: a pretext to test, as we sometimes do, the use of a new word— not a confession that finds the right words to express itself, but rather what is summoned by the desire to use certain words, to write in a certain way: a language playground, as diaries so frequently are.

I could recount in animal terms the terror I experienced before the imminent indiscretion, the moment the head flashes hot and the hands go cold, in the space between spoonfuls of soup. Grandma Lúcia was in this regard the opposite of a terrorist; she provided comfort from our fears and alleviated our fatigue, whisking us into our pajamas, opening the window, breaking our fever. How to touch upon these days filled with coming and going from school, chores, putting off the bath with its consistently protracted end, helping to set the table, watching the news, eating with elbows positioned pensively on the table, and listening to the soap until nine thirty at night? This nonliterary immortality where life proceeds without illness, without a single wicked incident save for a stuffy nose, laryngitis tempered with a steam inhaler. Perhaps this is the most appropriate image: long years, few in the end, spent breathing in warm vapors with a towel over one's head as the water cools—and sweating. This is what I've been needing recently, a half hour of my childhood steam baths, the only fitting tribute, but even this much requires a stuffy nose.

There were those who would say that I got whatever I wanted from my father, a blond-haired, prematurely bald young man who in past lives had been the blondest kid in the neighborhood, the child-elect to play Baby Jesus for a Beira nativity scene, the boy I see in a family photo album pushing a bassinet full of dolls—a boy in the hands of witches, as I'd learn to say years later. On the day in '82 when I was born in the Luanda Maternity, that little blond boy had grown up to be a young man with a full beard and chaotic curls in his hair. Eight years on, ours were simple pleasures: apple TriNaranjus, which I can be seen sipping through a straw in a historic photograph from Cascais, roast chicken and beefsteak dinner. The photograph of the TriNaranjus lies in an old box that I return to over and over again. Very little is required, in the end, to construct a history. I was proud at the thought that I had a passport, that I had been to Lisbon, where my school friends never set foot, a place that, in my head, barely stretched beyond the Parque Eduardo VII, with the notable exception of the Feira Popular theme park, where I always delighted in the thrill of the Ferris wheel on its way to the ground, the impression it gave of being moved by the wind. My father would take me to ride the pony and I would feign bouts of dizziness. Magic mirrors revealed how I would one day look, in an astonishing sequence that consoled me. It was during one of these outings that we were approached on a Lisbon street where we strolled hand in hand, and were asked whether we were related, my father and I, the inquiry laden with an odious curiosity.

Still oblivious to my bountiful head of hair, I walked with my father through the Praça da Figueira one Saturday night. I had developed a way of dashing to and fro, sprinting in a half crouch above the grates capping the running sewage water, out in front of the Pastelaria Suíça. In a black-and-white photograph, I'm dancing with a rain hat in the middle of the square, silhouetted against the night, glowing as I exclaim, "Look at me!" with the exuberance, now gone, that characterized me at that time, later to be replaced by the muttering with which I accompany these lines. The hair is there, a mane; I must not have brushed it when I woke up. I recovered this photograph this year, from atop a piece of furniture my paternal grandparents had in their living room: a mosaic of images of all of us, children, grandchildren, great-grandchilden, weddings, graduations—not a single baptism in my generation, except mine. On a shelf, a photograph of Grandma Lúcia and her brothers as children, in Seia, next to books about the Second World War, one of Grandpa Manuel's obsessions that I learned to apprehend as crypto-Judaism, of which he never uttered a word. He would say "Leningrad" with the gravitas with which my grandmother, clinging to a silvery Portuguese, used to say "sitting room."

I discovered that in the sitting room of my grandparents' house in Luanda, the small room where my aunts would listen to the exploits of their future sisters-in-law, all of them secretly smoked, barring Grandpa from entering by taking turns standing next to the door in nothing but their underwear, an image he ran from like it was the Devil. No one spoke of sex at this home in Portugal, though I did help Dona Lurdes fold underwear and Grandpa's socks into fun little rolls. He would lock himself in the bathroom for hours on end, "doing his toilette."

At his nightstand, he always kept a photograph of my engimatic great-grandmother, an unmistakable Jew. The photograph accompanied him for at least the thirty years in Florida-on-Oeiras. My great-grandmother lives on in the eyes and noses of a few aunts, above all in her childlike features, rediscovered in photographs and videos from when they were still just Viennese girls lost in Mozambique, distant cousins of the soft strands at the base of my neck. A few months back, I asked two different people the name of this Jewish lady and obtained divergent answers, a premonitory divergence. In the picture, my great-grandmother Conceição or Josefina has a fin-de-siècle hairstyle molded to the nape of her neck with a comb, her head lilting ever so slightly, her gaze peering off into the void, drama personified.

Conceição or Josefina was raised in Castelo Branco, the only daughter of a doctor who was a widower and a Mason. What's known is that she played piano, spoke French, wrote verse, and came attached to a fortune, a fact that didn't escape my great-grandfather, an army officer of humbler origins who lost her to cancer in the prime of life, then remarried nine months later. In Mozambique, Grandpa Manuel would take over her afternoons at the piano, forcing his children to listen to music all afternoon, teaching them to identify the different instruments of the orchestra, as he would do with his grandchildren in Oeiras, whenever he still cared to have company. The rest of the time, these afternoons of solitary music during my childhood—vestige of the girl from Castelo Branco that would show me that music isn't mere ornament but an occupation unto itself (Manuel was averse not to elevator music but to the very idea of background music, soundtracks)—were for him an umbilical matter and strictly private.

Today I think of my Great-Grandma Conceição or Josefina as a steadfast tuba, the bass that my untrained ear identifies most easily. What is there to say of the other clarinet, at moments faint, at others strident, that was my Macanese great-great-grandmother, the spouse of a celebrated colonel in Macau to whom we owe the almond-shaped eyes of our childhood, in my case further accentuated by the braids tugging at my forehead, but which I also find in my Portuguese cousins who inherited my Grandma Lúcia's hair? Manuel never wanted to hear a word of this clarinet; he considered it trivial, in keeping with the distant manner of a man who kept his origins in check like a maestro silencing musicians with his hands, raising his chin ever so slightly or forming a theatrical cross with his arms.

Our family's Judaism was silenced not only by the war, which, as the story goes, Manuel had followed to the sound of the Orquestra Caravana at the old Cinema Condes in Restauradores, but above all by the Catholicism of my Grandma Lúcia, whom he claimed to fall for upon seeing her descend a staircase in Seia, where he'd gone to work on the Serra da Estrela hydroelectric plant before he set off for Mozambique. Owner of a dogmatic sensitivity ("Your grandmother is a very sensitive person," my grandfather would say to me, the most important lesson of my life), my Grandma Lúcia, who had studied theology at Covilhã, raised only atheists, some of whom I managed to startle with the occasional agnostic outcry, an "oh God," an ancient appeal in the face of distress that came from the gut. Hers was a sentimental Catholicism that allowed her to accept others as they were with unimpeachable grace. She taught me to leave the Sunday roast in the oven before going to Mass, and how to pray the rosary. We would eat frozen fish at a dining table, surrounded by *Last Suppers*. On our way out of this gathering of catechists—a gathering of heads of hair, dim enough as they were, in a poorly lit basement where, at the end, they would allow me to join them for afternoon tea—we would wait for her, my grandfather and I, with what I recall as a sense of absolute security that could describe this entire period.

On Sundays after Mass, Grandpa would pick us up at the Church of Nova Oeiras, whose graying monseigneur we addressed on friendly terms and whom I then ascertained to be the only priest in existence. It's to my grandmother that I owe my baptism, at eleven years of age, an event for which I was unremitting in my preparation. My mother brushed my hair into three little buns held in place by three ribbons. I remember how, without my knowing it, my grandmother requested that the church choir sing my favorite hymn, which, on my way up to the baptismal font during Eucharist, left me stirring with the emotion she had transmitted to me and which was the form of her belief; not the easy, spontaneous tear, but the wisdom to bear the tear as it welled, brought forth by emotion and a knot in the throat that, though accompanied by pain, is a source of renewal. She rarely mentioned the Old Testament, I realize now: our life began after the Gospels, which was in fact true.

I tended not to pester Grandma Lúcia with questions about Jesus. When it came to my father's youthful beards, the fourth-floor neighbor's flowing mane, was my life not that of a curious little child called into His arms? It was. Did He not live there in our building, going out to the beach in the afternoon with a surfboard beneath his arm, stopping by as we learned to ride a bike, giving us a smack upside the head, saying to me, "That's quite the hair, little one!" and getting in a scuffle with the doorman, a balding hunter who gave me fried frog legs to try, to which I would always respond, "Ack"? Was it not Him there in the refrigerator and in the peanut-butter toast of the foreign-looking couple opposite us, two doctors who'd recently arrived from Alabama; in the attic of the Barbies on the sixteenth floor; at Dona Mena's, the hairdresser on three, she of the indelible ponytail? Why wouldn't Jesus be among the middle-class households of Oeiras, so abstemiously cared for and inconsonant with the rat's nest that so often set me in stark relief, my hair on end, heretical, scratched at with a hand spotted by felt-tip pens? (I always made a mess.)

My grandfather hated it when my grandmother cut her hair. He harbored an earnest hatred for Dona Esperança of the perms and the "old hen trims," as he called the elderly women's hairstyles. Grandma Lúcia brushed her hair to the back, reinforcing it with hairspray, and sometimes wrapped it inward toward her chin. He always abominated old age, my Grandpa Manuel. He would talk to me of "my friends," the young women who hosted programs on Galavisión and RAI Uno whose lipstick glimmered across the screen. "Did you see your friend there, Grandpa?"

"Yeah, I saw her."

The twentieth century would come to a close in 2014, the year my grandfather died. In the apartment in Oeiras, now empty, I follow the trail of electric wires that he ran beneath the hallway rug with the idea of installing satellite dishes and high-fidelity systems. The apartment served as my Portuguese grandfather's workshop. He would spend afternoons seated at the table, working out his calculations amid a pile of papers and bank statements. He would write *Paid* on all the bills, which piled up, to my grandmother's chagrin. In his free time, he would listen to music behind closed doors, marking the tempo with his chin. At such moments, he resembled his Jewish mother, the dramatic gaze into the void.

He once explained to me that it wasn't always a bad thing to abandon something halfway, telling me about Schubert's *Unfinished Symphony*, which he showed me in an attempt to pry me from the clutches of the *lambada* ("Grandpa, check out this dance!"), but I hadn't yet discovered the solace in the incomplete, preferring to make my peace with successive frustrations on my way toward objectives, pulling out problems and hair at the root, transforming the shame brought on by the whole matter into the matter itself. I remember us, late one Sunday afternoon, in a sacred ritual, throwing out the pile of newspapers bought that week and scattered around the house. "We're filtering through newspapers," we would tell the others, checking the dates. I remember sitting quietly after lunch to watch the stock market report on television; I remember Filipa Vacondeus, the "girl with no manners" who would grab her food with her hands; Grandma laughing at the Comendador Marques de Correia, whose jokes I could never find funny; the stale bread my grandfather would peck at as he waited for dinner; my well-cultivated aversion to the "Boliqueime Vampire," as Grandpa Manuel referred to the prime minister at the time. In the vases where Lúcia collected violets, today there are plants that died a decade ago. Two *Last Supper*s and a *Supper at Emmaus* head for the trash can reeking of tobacco. Below here, on the fifth floor, for a long time you could see an antenna glued to the parapet of the veranda off the living room—the insane idea of some engineer for whom duct tape was like Bactrim in the hands of my Grandpa Castro. I find a ruler from twenty-five years earlier in the very same drawer. The house is empty, the bathrooms adapted to the necessities of old age, the fear of losing one's balance, falling, breaking the pelvis. I snap some haphazard photographs and walk out of the apartment for the last time.

6

Only nearly twenty years after my strolls through Nova Oeiras with my mother did I learn the meaning of the word *peripatetic*. The term did not apply to us. There were neither masters nor disciples. We circulated through Oeiras, where she would spend vacations with me, staying at my grandparents' house, as though we were trying not to wake anyone. I would drag her by the arm. I took her to the Centro Comercial Europa, to Senhor Jorge's yarn shop, to the *tabacaria*, to the Café Londres, destinations she visited with the wonder of someone who had moved away, remarking at each new detail, which I could not, due to habit, notice. We would trade a few asides about hair; she would pick little pills from my clothing and wipe the sleep from my eyes. She waited while I took flight aboard a mechanical Maya the Bee found near the door of one café. We would pass by the entrance to my school, where I would point out my classroom windows. She would grab corn on the cob from the side of the road, and we'd continue on. In my mother's eyes, my neighborhood was disappearing with each passing year. She had spent her youth in Luanda, but each time she returned to Lisbon more and more of an adult. Strangely, I didn't think of her as the young woman she still was, but as a person without any age at all. She was me, come back to Oeiras twenty years on. Giving her my hand, dragging her through my routines, I tried to respect her somnambulism, though the landscape gradually added to her worries about me, revealing itself renewed, changed. "Ah! Now they've got a café here," she'd say to me, "Dona Esperança is so old," all as we walked, exactly like an emigrant who'd arrived for her August vacations: "Now it's *your* turn to show me Oeiras." Our stroll was an exam about my daily routine. I would show off, proposing shortcuts. These strolls were characterized, as I said, by the fact that they were not lessons; they were more like when a person shows another some work she's had done at her house. I took her with me to look at storefront windows, told her what I wanted her to buy me as I didn't dare do with anyone else, but it was all akin to guiding an amnesiac through the dark. The neighborhood refused to be roused, casting us about on the same order as previous years with its implacable gusts.

"That's right. And your cousin Marta?" she would ask me. "She's good, she got married," and we turned another corner. "Grandma Lúcia walks down there," she would continue, her interjection addressing the changed landscape, as though, faced with the life of things, all that came to her mind was the life of those we knew. I responded with the distractedness of someone dedicated to a task, worried I might get us lost and allowing, for a second, my fear to be noted. "You see! We're already lost, where is *this* going to take us?" Perhaps the Oeiras of '89 was nothing more than one long waking dream: the Modelo supermarket, wearing down the same old faces standing behind the cash register; the rooftop Contera satellite dishes that appeared in all of my drawings; the still-youthful palm trees of the Cesário Verde Promenade and the elementary school farther on, like some feudal estate house where we were vassals; the urbanization projects still under way; the tiny church with its white paint, today encircled by a bike lane. These strolls were the closest things we had in life to resisting temptation in the desert, despite frequently crossing paths with neighbors along the way.

It was, at that time, normal for us to begin eating late. I would wait, I'm still waiting, for her to finish her prayer, her implorations, in several dead languages, for our forgiveness, the end of Ebola, a neighbor's fertility, or the arrival of a much-awaited phone call, whether we were at home or on the esplanade, in Luanda, Lisbon, or somewhere else. Having given thanks for the stew, we would dig in, ignoring the fat accumulating on the surface, a decent picture of our condition as supplicants, and of my mental state while I waited for her to finish, opening and closing her eyes for no other reason than to try to measure time. Her closed eyes are, however, a faulty timepiece.

She never got caught up in the mechanics of prayer, the way those who don't know how to pray do. Prayer was, above all, fertile terrain for improvisation, where she didn't trouble herself with vain questions of whether we have a duty to restrain ourselves when we ask something of God. I would ask myself, meanwhile, why Jesus would not tell those who asked Him how to pray to improvise, a thought that did nothing to allay my impression that Our Father, a prayer for the illiterate, contained very little knowledge next to the loquacity to which my mother always accustomed me. As a little girl, I felt at such moments the primordial sense of shame that we feel only for our parents and for which our parents are forgiven by their children. I didn't experience this shame as my own failing, though she would call me *Mom* and ask me for advice when I was but eight, nine, ten years old. Today, I can hear her praying in a state of rapture and I feel grateful when I note in her a gift common to certain loners, that of taking a break from themselves, a feat that has eluded my dedicated efforts. It is she who is absent from her pleas, absorbed in what she is saying, on a continuous retreat from the senses, as though the prayer were praying her.

We spent very little time together. We saw each other when she would come to Portugal, or else I would go to Luanda for fifteen days spent alternating between joy and timidness. If we were in Lisbon, we would trot her somnambulism around Oeiras or, grabbing a streetcar, we would climb the Rua da Prata, stopping mid-ascent for a croissant, and then we'd continue up to the Parque Eduardo VII where a gypsy woman would tell our fortunes. If we were in Luanda, I would spend the afternoons at the balcony window, showing off my ever-changing hair; or I would go to the corner baker, sprinting on my errand, fearing I'd be found out and trying to adjust my accent when speaking with the shopkeepers. We were two strangers, even if she did towel me off and dress me after the bath, teach me to put lotion on my body as she commented on the way my pubis looked, and despite the fact that one of us was responsible for the other. My mother saw us both through the lens of Providence, in whose shadow we are the tiniest of images, and I made my yearning for her tiny, too, drawn as she was by the daily obligations that continued uninterrupted by vacation, the times she had to work, the showers taken with a tin cup in the interludes between water shortages, the trash collection done by a handful of street kids she never tired of feeding.

The wonder, then, was in her showing me that such responsibility was a passing circumstance; that we were both beneath the aegis of a higher power, which I only glimpsed as the shadow fleeing down the apartment hallway where I was too afraid to wander alone during these summers in Luanda. Even if the foreignness of these habits, to which we dedicated ourselves as though they were in fact habits, was equivalent to making us two strangers who shared a rented house, my mother made me feel we were residents of a welcoming home. The landlord would look after us, would look after me, no matter that he didn't make me feel at home. The question was not, for this reason, one of being worthy of his visit to our abode, but one of learning, through his insistence on these visits, that we were the real visitors. The landlord made it clear to us that we didn't belong, revealing the drama all renters face and laying bare the formality behind all visits. Despite experiencing each fear and joy as my own, my spirits were stipulated by contract. The tenant's formality toward her shelter, I realize today, is many a time the shortest path to her forgetting about herself, the thankless and blessed position I had sensed in my mother's prayerful self-effacement.

This process of becoming a stranger in one's own house, an estrangement essential to our place on this earth, would nevertheless be the condition that rendered possible the expansion of my mind, which was then broadening against my mother, as though gaining territory against an oppressive skeleton, on account of her being the way in which God appeared in my life. The house she taught me to regard with distrust was myself, though it might have appeared to whoever saw the two of us together that we weren't bound by mere contingency. God was the stranger who taught us to become strangers to ourselves, ironically lifting the threadbare veil that was my vague notion of ownership and showing me just how precarious it was to refer to myself as "me." Our meeting provided the means for me to take a leap, as my father would say to me after going to pick me up at the Acroporto da Portela, when my vacation in Luanda had come to an end. A leap made inside my head, and not in shoe size—that is what I owe to my mother.

Taking this leap was not, however, a way of growing closer to myself but a form of watching my head grow distant, the same way a kite might flee my grasp; and God's role in my life was prolonged in the way I would learn to stand on ceremony with my thoughts. Our summers would mark the occasion of a decapitation: my head running off to grow far out of sight, and with it my hair. The distance that separated my mother and me was the only observable sign that my head had become unmoored. It was this she spoke of on the telephone during those decapitated years when we rarely saw each other, each time she asked about my hair, as though in some indirect way I was given to understand by her questions that she wanted to know whether I'd found myself yet. Our decapitated years are our happiest years, even if the idea of our being mere tenants of ourselves, my mother's life philosophy and her reserve of enthusiasm, brings a smile to our lips. She would, throughout the years, make the journey alone back to a room of her own, returning to the solitude of individual worship. It was then that I realized that children are only one aspect of their mothers, an aspect whose importance the years sometimes make clear.

As a child, in a corner of my bedroom in the apartment that belonged to my Grandma Lúcia and Grandpa Manuel, I stashed plastic bags that I filled with toys and drawings that I wished to draw her attention to the next time we met, the luggage from a trip that we would one day take together and from which I hoped never to return. The most precious part of this collection was the way I retired these objects from daily use, stowing them away for her, stowing myself away for her: if some futile object grabbed my attention, it went into the plastic bag and not the toy basket.

I had my bags packed, happy though I was, a state that would last for many years. The life of the objects in my collection—the heads of dolls, a Bic ballpoint pen, a yo-yo split down the middle—was a parallel life, not life in Oeiras. I didn't take these bags from the corner of my bedroom on vacations to Luanda, though I told my mother about them, remarking, "Everything's ready." During the rest of the school year, my mother was the phantom at the breakfast table, enticed as I often was by my Grandma Lúcia to finish my milk, long since cold, on the promise that she would call me. I would then settle in at the window with glass in hand, commenting on the weather as though someone were listening, and, bringing the glass to my mouth, pour the milk out the window, dirtying my pajamas with chocolate and promptly declaring, "All done!" What I was preparing for with those plastic bags in the corner of my room in the apartment in Oeiras (where after a few minutes any fascinating object became nothing more than trash) was a future as a homeless person, not a life with a family.

7

Childhood had a number of ethnic Carnaval celebrations in store for me. I can see myself in '88 with a feathered headband, a brown vest, and bangs, masquerading as an American Indian, thanks not to any choice or inclination of childhood Mila, but to the circumstance (which says so much about so many things in life) that it was the only mask available. In '89, my hair is once again forgotten beneath a headscarf, and I sport filigree earrings; someone had broken a rotten egg over my head, the scarf providing protection from the stench. In 1990, I'm seen dressed as a gypsy, and, the following year, I must have decided on my own to dress up as a vampire. In 1992, I took the form of a premonitory scarecrow, making the most of my wiry hair as natural straw, atop which sat a tiny hat, also made of straw and disproportionate in size to my hair, for the birds to land on—why go on? That's where Carnaval, never a happy occasion for me, came to a definitive close. How lonely my hair has been all these years!

Surviving this period of uprooting and neglect is the memory of deliberate attempts at new hairstyles, in contrast to what had previously been a complete disregard for my hair, in fact, a disregard, deliberate or infantile, for the fact that I had hair at all—perhaps a family curse, rather than my own curse, rather than a failing. I understand it today, as I pass through relatives' apartments in Oeiras, through the hair, either colored or graying, of my paternal aunts, Christmas-themed earthenware ceramics on display in the middle of spring. I reencounter the objects of my childhood: the same pictures hanging in the same haphazard spots. No one has straightened them all these years, or so it seems. These houses are a reflection of my hair, even if visiting them is a journey to a Galápagos of human nature, such is the diversity of temperaments: the austerity of some and the laissez-faire of others in mutual antagonism, culinary talent and a complete aversion to the kitchen, the art of slumber turned others' insomnia, a shared appreciation for household pets. It is not the daily life of my hair but the variations in my way of caring for it—with zeal at one turn, with carelessness at another, always a contradiction—that my family homes reveal to me with their owners, their dogs, their cats.

In 2011, spurred on by a displeasure I could no longer deny, I cut my hair to forget it even further. Of course, I explained this forgetting to myself in simple, practical terms: washing and getting around, etc. What I can't do, I would later admit to myself, is forget this hair without also forgetting myself and plowing forward while leaving myself behind, like two people who lose sight of one another at a street market. In the aftermath of this last cut, the desire to know my hair's history had its beginnings. The primary reason would reveal itself over time, upon the realization, ineffable though it was, that the place where I was born —only to grow up far away—was returning to me as an oblique but constant place of interest. At the same time Luanda would come to me, I found myself going back to Oeiras, in another change of neighborhood: there I was once again in the streets where Grandma Lúcia would take her perm on parade, my hand in hers, the streets we'd take to Sunday Mass or for a summer stroll after dinner, at a time when everyone did so.

I had short-cropped hair and found myself at home the day I woke up yearning for myself, but a yearning for someone I had never been, for two or three streets in Luanda, for a stereotype: a yearning, my God, for the human caricature that I could have been, an exoticism. When it comes to this Mila who doesn't exist, the person I've become sees her imagination walled in by an

exasperating ignorance of Africa. From where I'm standing, this yearning could not be filled in by any sort of
return. Where would I go? Find myself where? It wasn't
merely this change of address that, carrying me back to
the suburbs of my Portuguese childhood, brought me,
ironically, a yearning for Angola. It was also having no-
ticed, thanks to exhaustive evidence, that I'm not like the
people central to my life, there's something fundamental
that separates us that goes much deeper than our hair.
Though it's hard to admit, the enviable environment of
equality in which I had the good fortune to be educated
in Portugal kept me from something important that I'm
now trying to remember: a clear notion of the differences
that separate me from those among whom I happened to
grow up, those who were, in fact, the people who taught
me to notice the significance of the differences whose absence I regret.

This book is written in an imperfect tense of courtesy.
Courtesy is the virtue reserved for the ineffable, as though
the only thing left to do were to stand on ceremony with
those things that are familiar to me. This is the formal
ghost that haunts me: the fear that the best means are to
expose the means. As with the scarecrow from '92, exposing the means is a way of scaring up answers. So then
what the scarecrow drives out is reality and its characters,
the tools of biography and its thorny poetics. "Who is
Mila?" "I am" doesn't quite fit. Hair is cut and grows back,

prolonging a series of cycles, but that is nothing more than a path to extinction. Each cycle of my hair is only a cycle of the story of my hair. Will it be me ("the true me"?) who gives the story meaning by telling it? I ask myself how to maintain my distance if I'm rustling around in memory, but distance, I quickly realize, is a condition of memory, not an ethics. All the past is a close-range satellite.

For a long time I thought that, according to a suitable notion of integrity, sharing Mila's story would be a fraudulent act. I thought that she would be perceived as a stock black woman. I realize now, however, that only for me is the person I never was a caricature. Belonging to a minority consists not only of borrowing from our intimate iconography; it consists of erasing all singularity that might exist, not in the life we have lived, but in the life we have not. There appears to be little of the collective in the story of this borrowing. Rather, it resembles a personal inaptitude for better remembering the people we never came to be. Memory is a demagogue: it doesn't allow us to choose what we see; it thrives on the temptation to make less of the people we *were not*. I confess that I forgot, I erased, I dispelled the invisible. I filed away the salons and the women in those salons. The record of my forgetting is distinctly Portuguese. There, one can find the outskirts of Lisbon in the scant details of my juvenilia, pigeons, an invalid woman and the poor, white clothing in the wind, madwomen at the window, and one Elephant Man. How to remember the person I never was as I would anyone else?

"Are you still talking about your hair, Mila?" Determined to discover who I am, like a surprise in the middle of my journey, an unforeseen epiphany, I suddenly find myself entangled in my own particularity. I assumed that I would dissolve into others, losing myself to the obscurity that I intended to rescue them from, but now I'm left with only my own idea of my hair, a retrospective fog hovering over my identity. Now, it seems to me that the only admissible notion of integrity is that of honoring not the person I have been but the person I consider myself never to have become. It is the stock black woman who today deserves my deference. How to be worthy of her? I don't know how to do my hair on paper without this story slipping from my grasp.

8

In a book, I come across images of ruins. I leaf through the sequence. I experience it as a family photo album. Castles, control towers, prisons, aqueducts, abandoned pools: *us* in our childhood photo albums. What's common to the images is not the way they reflect a collective tradition of neglect, but the way that surviving monuments present themselves as living pairs belonging to a single familiar pathway. Such are my feelings for each one that flashes before me: in a single city, there's no room for more than one water park in ruins. In one image, a field has over-taken the ruins of a castle. In another, a slide empties out into what was once a community pool. Would that we could find new uses for the equipment of the past, turn a cane devoured by woodworms into a flute or a baroque-style handrail; rediscover familiar traditions in the effects of time and nature; conflate neglect with artistic intent.

Such is the entire contents of what remains of what is gone. It's not the places we formerly inhabited and that today I find abandoned that assume the status of ruins. It is we who, though we've not been abandoned, survive like the only castle in a miles-wide radius: a sign that life once existed where today there's only dead grass, olive trees, and cork oaks. My damaged childhood photos—crammed into an old shoebox to slowly lose their color, in some cases gluing to one another—do not owe their survival to the cure of some documentarian. We cannot dispense with the rediscovery of ourselves as the product of the records that our neglect has relegated to a drawer, exactly as if we'd come to the realization that the purpose of the cure, of the restorer's zeal, was not that of zealously caring for the recorded materials themselves but for all that reaches us from what we have documented. As if the cure could cure the individuals registered there, and not the medium through which they live on. We cannot deny that our childhood has changed color, and that its coloring now is not the sepia occasioned by the photograph but the sepia of our neglect.

In the photographs, I see a temple or a Roman bridge; a Moorish tower; catacombs; a Ford from the 1910s; one of the first light aircraft. This doesn't mean only that we coincide with what has endured, but that the life of the

past as we reencounter it corresponds to the monumental-
ization of what we experience as forgettable. What wasn't
worth remembering we've transformed into a monument,
as though dropping an ice cream on the ground, pulling
the hair back into a ponytail for a passport photo, or taking apart a bike were now our Ksar el-Kebir, our own
siege of Lisbon, our transatlantic crossing, our Tarrafal,
even as sieges, crossings, concentration camps, and battles
that we never saw coming make history. "We are making
history," I can hear us saying out loud, and I think that the
spirit of this phrase dwells in the antipodes of everything
we can learn during our lives.

When I was already an adult, I saw for the first time a
silent movie of my paternal grandparents in Mozambique
with their children, then still kids, climbing in and out
of a Peugeot like chicks chasing the mother hen. They
leapt into a pool made of rubber and then into an actual
pool where there are no black people to be found. At an
airfield, they salute the arrival of a general who is greeted
by indigenous tribes wearing traditional dress and waving
little flags; they read the newspaper in the shadow of the
papaya tree in their yard. This was in 1977. The movie's
transposition to DVD resulted in the film being sped up.
Images always followed by a cut: Beira, Venice, Lourenço
Marques, Fafe. Despite the Jewish features of most of the
children, on film my family face life flaunting the musical proclivities of the von Trapps, like a generation of

singers perennially at the brink of escaping persecution. The filmography of our fin-de-siècle Christmases in Portugal intrudes on our idea of who we are, as though we couldn't freely survive what we took for leisure. The movie we watched in 1990 portrayed us as we were in 1970 by showing us in the '40s. In the place of our stern looks, we were reborn musicians: this recompense straight from some artist's workshop—distance and its caprices—turning us into automatons, stripping away our souls.

My family's musicality in these silent movies is the product of the films' technical deterioration. Once again, it is as if the demands of chance made it possible to reveal the uniqueness in things, despite what ends up being only a partial representation of certain moments in their lives. The film's deterioration suppresses all the anguish, though we might lament seeing ourselves reduced to things. We are dead, I think as I watch us, the same way I would if I happened to reencounter a dead actor in one of the films.

And so we are reborn as the epiphany of an artist who found within this deterioration of his medium—and despite the high cost of any epiphany—a purpose, a new possibility for beauty, as though the stage where our lives play out were the stuff, albeit insignificant, of someone else's effort; as though the papaya tree of '77 were one of many tiny trees in a maquette, arranged according to the necessity and inspiration of a meticulous architect; as if

the label on the bottle of TriNaranjus from our trip to
Cascais toward the end of 1980 were the whim of an ex-
hibitionist painter; as though the turquoise at the bottom
of the pool in the silent movie of my grandparents were
the result of a film restorer's precision; and the musical
enthusiasm of the von Trapps were the beginning of a
melody that some musician rescued from the noise made
by an old recording.

What I reencounter as a caricature of Mozambique is
nothing more than the way a film's technical deterioration resituates what has taken place, giving the impression that we have been determined, reflected by others,
like a little pile of dry leaves whose collapse strikes us as
the will of the leaves themselves: like Chinese shadow
puppets of each one of us.

The characters' zeal in these nostalgic movies of
Mozambique; the colors of the people and the contours
of their summer fashions; the movement of cars and the
resignation of their newsies and drivers and, more than
anything, all of its counterfeit music; our nostalgia today
not for what was but for what we remember—everything
is a byproduct of the deterioration of some material,
which assails not only individual families without names
or private albums, but barges into all frames, all record-
ings, all forms of records. Castles, control towers, prisons,
aqueducts, abandoned swimming pools: the *us* in our
childhood photo albums. Is it really us? We who can't

remember having walked so swiftly, having smiled so
carefreely, having taken a dive from such heights, having
done our hair with such dedication; we who resurfaced
sick, morose, joyful, weary, defeated, without remembering ever returning or being defeated, between what we
are and *this*, the deteriorated record silences us like a
sound-absorption blanket in whose layers we might still
manage to find a ray of virtue, a dignified version of each
of us: a monument. How inadequate it is to say that we
were making history when all that we managed to hear
from each moment was merely the fury of some Chinese
shadow-puppet theater actor's devotion.

Never again be ashamed of who you are, I read in a book.
This phrase comes back to me as I watch the movies, as
though they were showing the life of a single person, and
without it ever being clear why this is the appropriate
subtitle for all of these actors and their zeal. In order to
never again be ashamed of who we are, it is necessary
that we be on our way to becoming something. At such
time we can become aware of the possibility of chasing
after certain designs, as if before we didn't realize it was
possible that a certain thing could serve as our aspiration. That is when we recognize it as a personal objective,
with the same sense of wonder with which we discovered
beauty in deterioration. Vocations frequently sneak up
on us as epiphanies. The company of others serves to put
them in perspective. It occurs to me what things might be

like if life were the search for truth. If in the face of what remains we are, at best, the beauty that is found in trash as it decomposes, as appears to happen to any memory, not as a result of the documentalist's dream but of nightmares about his own absolute expendability. To seek the truth seems as inglorious as trying to kill the figure of a Chinese shadow-puppet eagle. As with dreams, in the face of his epiphanies, the documentalist discovers himself in the face of the documents before him, as when we, appearing to ourselves in our dreams, discover that we are still the same, despite the shaggy beards, the college diplomas that mark the beginning of a conversation with the people we've become. At the time when none of us gave a thought to our hair, Mozambique was sweaty, licentious, languid.

9

One of the few photographs in which my hair appears tamed was taken by a Will Counts in September 1957. This story of my hair is its caption and its salvaging. It is perhaps strange that, being a self-portrait, it was captured by another person, at the entrance to Central High School in Little Rock, Arkansas, long before I was born, and would become a symbol of the struggle for civil rights in the United States. Stranger still and harder to explain is the fact that I am all of the people in that portrait at once.

Not that this photograph symbolizes some particular episode in my life. It is foremost an X-ray of my soul. My soul is the deceptively poised figure of Elizabeth Eckford in the foreground and the insatiable hatred of the multitude trailing her in the background. My fear is

IMAGE CREDIT: Will Counts Collection: Indiana University Archives

focused entirely in the contraction of the hand and fore-
arm muscles, holding my notebook by the spine, afraid
of dropping it and being swallowed up by all those girls.
All the violence of the portrait converges on my clenched
teeth haranguing a complete stranger. I am the curious
bystanders, hair to a T, who trail behind just to have a
little fun. It is the portrait of a self-persecution and the
daily struggle to achieve indifference.

The photograph of Little Rock gets me thinking about
a certain Mónica in my ninth year, a girl whose face was
scarred from a late case of chicken pox and who often
declared she would prefer to abort than to give birth to
a black child; or Sofia at the Central, where I learned to
enjoy the taste of coffee—a sullen girl who worked the
afternoon shift and was always yawning behind the counter, who, waiting on all the other diners with a look of
disgust, saved her segregationist repugnance for when she
brought my bill. It's mysterious that I shouldn't recognize
them among the white girls in the portrait. I don't recognize them because the white girls in the portrait are
nothing less than myself in miniature, *little rock*, the *mulata das pedras*. I see now that I am the persecuted and the
persecutor, the disfigured, disfiguring myself.

This image captures the supremacist in me, the tor-
mentor's essence that ruins my days, as much as there's
nothing or no one to attack me or who has attacked me
except myself; the supremacist implicit in the reticent,

wounded timidity of so many headfuls of wiry hair that I encounter around Lisbon, a timidity much more justi- fied than mine because, all things considered, all forms of timidity were in my case always a natural privilege and not a reaction to circumstance. This supremacist is the idea, found in each of my brothers, that your timid- ity (which no one notices) is a burden that ought to be purged, in an attempt to find, as we walk through this world, a precise combination of disdain, meekness, and expansivity.

He whispers to us, telling us not to make eye con- tact with the police, not to complain too much on the road, not to take up the reserved seats in empty buses, to step aside on a city sidewalk, to, when dealing with important matters, change our accents on the telephone, to disappear from the hallways where we truly do disap- pear, amid apologies and innumerable silences, leaving the slippery floor as a vestige, to forget the Story of Our Hair, though there's not a single sound here outside— nothing, not a thing.

Seemingly tying my peaceful stroll to Elizabeth's, this supremacist eludes all the known definitions, though he remains even when he's stopped his roaring. He was very much alive in my Grandpa Castro, who railed against the "blackies" on the bus. He was very much alive in the initial reaction of every single hairdresser—black or white—to the texture of my hair. He's not a defining

excuse but a brazen narrator. I can hear him clearly. He
is the italics from conversations at the corner café that
startle me as though the subject were me. "I had to get rid
of my *black* skirt: it got ruined in the washer"; "Look at
the *black* smoke that motorbike is leaving behind," say the
old ladies amid a clatter of saucers, teacups, forks, knives,
spare change. I look over my shoulder in search of clues;
the conversation proceeds; I can see it has nothing to do
with me. The raging girls in the photo are the nervous
tremor (which brings me shame) when a black man on
the streetcar answers the phone, speaking loudly. "Shhh:
pipe down," they say to me, I say to him, I say to myself.
"Can't you see the others?" They accost me at the mirror
when I'm getting ready to go out, convincing me repeatedly that a pair of gold hoop earrings are ethnic, and for
this reason vulgar, and so I set them aside. They make
me selflessly prepared for the insult that always greets me
when I step out into the street, even if the only sound
there is of dogs barking beneath the rain. Every day, I
mobilize myself for what is almost never more than a
swell of clouds, the wicked sneer of the racist past, my
genuine fears revealed to be quixotic. The raging girls are
the silent cause of the discretion of the "good girl" I've
become. Their italics assumed the force of nature: curly
hair made straight.

10

At age fourteen I awoke from the negligence of my hair to a drawing given to me by a certain suitor in which I appeared nude and hunched over myself, braids undone and falling down my back. The work of a Senegalese woman in Algés, these braids were an entire day in the making, an experience memorable for the bowl of boiling water where, after the woman had finished, I submerged my braids to curl the tips of my extensions. My suitor envisioned me nude, hair long and flowing, which sent me running. After he gave me the drawing, I ran home, and, for a long time, I avoided him, not without curiosity. One day I tried to discover where he'd landed. He'd become a salesman, a family man, something no one could have anticipated.

I was reborn with my new hair extensions—which had never been so long—with a natural air that, at a distance, perplexes me. Within me, I found all the knowledge peculiar to long hair, a way of putting it behind the ears that lasted between each sporadic cut, a natural movement of the shoulders that quickly became a tic, an obsession with rolling the tips around my fingers. This collection of latent gestures, standing by for what never came to be, was in my case the exact opposite of an amputated limb's enduring life: the prehistory of a nonexistent organ for which we had always been waiting without knowing just how much we missed it. Like my hair extensions, made long in a matter of minutes, I took a leap forward.

It is in the part of this story yet to be written, the part concerning the renting out of castles and construction sites to event organizers, that, with comical marksmanship, in the middle of the '90s, I gained a sense of pride in my braids. They would sway as I danced, often the only person relatively sober among hundreds of the high; alerted, as I hit puberty, to the dangers of drugs thanks to the shock therapy administered to the tune of the spirit of that time: the lame who stepped out of the trolley in Campolide with perfect stride; a campaign against chemical dependence that would be conducted at my preparatory school when I was eleven years of age and a sense of responsibility that was nothing more than well-timed cowardliness. We'd wake up at five in the morning to the parties that for others were the climax of their nights; we would grab the "night train" and take it to the Clímax club in Jardim Constantino, a girlfriend and I who dreamed of becoming groupies for a band of slackers who attended raves and after-hours parties and met up at the door of a gambling parlor in the vicinity. No one tells this story because there were no observers who were not also participants. Of those who participated, there's no one left.

It's dirty, the ethnography of that time. At the raves, in the dark, observers found they were natives, native observers. I would repeat to myself that I was there for the music, trying not to lose track of the stranger wearing a top hat: an eccentric who made the rounds of the buildings, his obsolete form of assistance that of a cane, perhaps from Cacém. Was he looking for someone, that master of ceremonies, impervious to the chamber of loops: a visiting undertaker, perhaps? To follow the undertaker with my gaze was to admit I'd fallen prey, though I swore I knew him from somewhere. To the other side, in front of me, a sweaty neck, making me worry. Drink some water, dummy, I would think, a poor concerned godmother; behind me, in an open-air courtyard, negotiations on the sly over ecstasy, conducted with the gallantry peculiar to the black market. At my side, someone was sticking their tongue out. Beneath the noise, consigned to silence, an acrobatic approach prompted by our need to focus in order to let ourselves go, we were alone. Going to a rave

only appeared to be a group endeavor. I would say goodbye to my friends at the door and locate within the noise
a cell of my own, synchronizing my heart to the rhythm.
Amid the mystery of other hearts joy was nowhere to be
found, but rather the obstacle of solitude each time we
lost grasp of ourselves. Losing ourselves is nonetheless a
noble aspiration and not an effect. No one was looking
for the heart of the undertaker lost in his funereal rounds,
for which he would have no explanation. It was the omnipresent undertaker who never let me rest: the trace of
surveillance I could never shake.

Much of what I know of the Portuguese countryside
I learned from those years I spent with friends crossing Ribatejo, the north, and when we went alone to the
Algarve, in '97, for the Festival Neptunus, on the money
we'd earned tacking on bar codes at a warehouse in Sintra,
under the careful watch of a tyrannical redhead. At lunch,
we would eat with a group of older ladies who had been
there twenty-seven years and some stern-looking triplets
with their hair pulled back. On the trip to Albufeira, that
same year spent at the warehouse, riding on a train full of
soldiers who'd been challenged by the other ravers to try
poppers, they repeatedly whispered in my ear that I had
"really crazy" hair. My hair was no longer "that hair." Two
guys began to kiss, but they still didn't know each other
any better for it, nor did they care to. Everyone back then
claimed to be sixteen and took into account that from

two o'clock in the morning onward, there would be no more water in the faucets at the club.

At my friend Cátia's place, where we would get ready to go out, and where the host would wear to school the same clothes she wore out at night, I would help fry rissoles for lunch. Hers was a family of medical assistants, truck drivers, pregnant teenagers, and academic failures. One afternoon when I saw her leaving the shower, she dried off in front of me, wiping her privates with a towel and staring at the blood that had appeared there. Where had Oeiras been lost along the way, the decorous sitting room? It was Cátia who took me to the Bairro de Santa Filomena for the first time. We were looking for a relative of hers who lived in an abandoned house; we stood there yelling at the door, shouting, "Anybody home?" We yelled at the ruin, a condemned dwelling on top of a hill, waiting for someone to show up. We had come to claim child support. I can still see us today, yelling at the top of the hill, Cátia hurling insults at the mute ruin in a rage whose origins were elsewhere.

My friends from this time: a blond-haired Rastafari who trafficked drugs; a black Rastafari who lived beneath the train tracks in Rio de Mouro, where one day I was greeted by his grandmothers, and who wanted to marry me; the boy who'd given me the drawing, ten years my senior, who, it was said, swallowed eight pills of ecstasy in a single night; the two sisters without the slightest resemblance who looked down to find lizards crawling out of the arms of the sofas at the Clímax; the boy from Camarate who swore he'd been the first person in Lisbon to wear checkered pants; his friend, who acted as if he were being forced to go to the parties; those who, without knowing a word of English, set off for London only to be barred at the door of Ministry of Sound; those who spent intermissions with their gaze to the ground, consumed by the etiquette of their trade, the transactions that left them crumpled receipts—I never again came across any of them, not in a metro station, nor any city bus, not a single café. I moved to another country, or they did, though only a few kilometers separated us. Once, after some years, I heard my name at the supermarket. It was one of them, and I introduced my husband. The man was straightening bottles on a shelf. These were the first people to boast of my hair.

During one of the three summers our friendship would last, I spent an afternoon with Cátia and her boyfriend at the beach at Carcavelos. Around my waist, I wore a waterproof gold chain. The beach was nothing more than a train station at the end of the line, where we found ourselves semi-nude, but still the same. I would shake my braids at the edge of the sea, a third wheel. Cátia was worried her boyfriend might get up from the towel and covered him with her own body. She whispered in my ear that he had "a hard-on," an expression I had never heard before. The boys and girls at the station would haul it together toward the sea, gazing at each other's asses and torsos, and dive into the water with high-flying somersaults, making waves for several feet, bothering the others. They threw pebbles for dogs to chase without heeding the children, smoked hashish in the shade as we read *Ragazza*, pushed and shoved one another in apparent skirmishes, fell asleep beneath the sun, ate a Magnum, swiped some sunglasses, asked our names, tried to get to know us, and, in the end, took the bus back home, harmless passengers along for the ride, sunglasses perched atop their baseball caps, their black skin spotted with salt marks the sea had left on their arms, their legs, their necks, marks that looked like some dermatological disease, bookish debris in which they'll never play a part.

One morning, on my way to an *after-hours* in Ericeira, at Saturday's, we grabbed a lift from a farmer who'd come along in a wagon. Today I think about us, seated on bales of hay, plastered with makeup, aloof to the beauty of the route, the mare's trot, our ears glued to a track entitled "Mannikohmium," pure noise. It was the only time I ever rode in a wagon. The next year, in '98, I left in the middle of a party asking myself how I'd ever managed to stand that song. It seemed like a decade had passed, but it was only three years of my life.

It's not essential that we know where we're going, and there are times we might feel lost or think there's something

wrong with us in some important way. Ambition, a
mighty powder keg that doesn't necessarily bring talent
with it and can even encourage mediocrity, guides some
of us with persistent fidelity. Ambition accompanied me
everywhere I went with a reserve of individuality that refused to be tarnished. Today, it nonetheless surprises me
when I think about the fate of those I encountered along
the way. Ambition warmed the hearts of some, and it was
futile for them in the way it is for me, perhaps. What
became of my companions from the '90s, the troupe of
striving traffic controllers, INEM ambulance drivers,
cruise ship burger-flippers, Continente checkout clerks,
girls who kept boys company, flight attendants, office
workers, biological engineers, chemists, classicists, solo
guitar players?

I don't know why I had to commit myself to the aim
of finding beauty in that which repels me, but I've given
in to the pressure to do so more out of consideration for
the authenticity of these projects than the allure of those
high school years. This authenticity reached its climax
in the energy my friends put into afternoon concerts,
emerging from the apathy of school biology labs. They
stretched out nude and played electric guitar on some
apartment terrace, interrupted by the sirens coming from
the cars of cut volunteer firemen, whose tender spectacle
of familial comedy I followed through a café window. In
the same stretch of August, they would turn their hoses

on one another, these firemen; they would piggyback the pudgy girls and flee the spurting water, their chests bare and beer bellies emerging from bulging ribs, a world where everyone is cousins and bravery is a family trait. Back on the terrace, our anti-family would drink orange vodka and smoke weed in the sun. At times, in a stroke of poetic inspiration when someone's parents were traveling, we allowed ourselves to stay awake until the sun rose over the terrace. When I look back at this family today, I can hear us telling tales about a man who kept a lion on the roof of a building in Lisbon's Bairro Azul, for which there is still photographic evidence. I took part in the ambition of my friends, terrace-top lions, ignoring all the ugliness of the city below, which, as we never tired of saying, would one day be picturesque. Adolescence was merely the exacerbation of what none of us ever wanted to become, as if for a few years we were allowed to be a lesser version of ourselves that could explode in our very hands. The ambition we experienced as a group at this time, which one day would put us in our place, was misplaced and fleeting. It wasn't yet the disease that my grandfather passed on to me, though it befell him, too.

Manuel convinced me, when I was little, that a luminous future awaited me, as perhaps is advisable to convince all children. What he gave me in those days, when he recited my infantile verses to the family and suggested I read Jules Verne, predicting a literary fate for me, were not means but ends. Only in the young is it possible to induce such daunting ambition. My grandfather abided by his predictions, which he feared he might not live to witness, and, for this reason, what he passed on to me was the condition of his own perpetuation, a blank check concerning his own future, not mine, despite the fact that the two of us did not draw a distinction. Ambition was a reciprocal blessing, and it could only be that way, as it's not something we can generate within ourselves. How unwarranted was my certainty that I had a luminous fate ahead of me, when, during the '90s or early 2000s, the nauseating daily life of Lisbon's dirty little alleyways rose up around me, the smell of urine, condoms, and dirty needles, empty plastic cups I'd also drunk from. What's for certain, ludicrous though it may seem, is that it has been ambition and not a sense of responsibility that's protected me throughout this journey. This was the idea my grandfather gleaned from my first quatrains, as though an old man's eternity could be foretold in the way a child rhymes the word *tide* with the word *petrified*. My childhood poems revealed my audience's future, not mine. Never had the two of us been so close to the life after death as in this fantasy of my Grandpa Manuel.

11

The worst hairdressers I've ever seen were two Congolese women at the Centro Comercial da Mouraria—either they were horribly ugly or time has transfigured them—their faces losing their pigment thanks to Mekako, an antiseptic soap used to lighten the skin. They worked weaves into my hair at breakneck speed over four hours and charged me a fortune, casting a disdainful gaze toward the white boyfriend I'd brought with me. The first two weaves fell apart just hours later, the moment I touched them. The two women belonged to the family of a man who had insulted me in the street, saying I must have learned to like white boys from my mother—forever ruining Lisbon for us. As a little girl, I'd learned to say *Tata Nzambi*, "Oh my God" in Lingala, an interjection, repeated by my mother, that crosses my mind at such moments. It was also thanks to her that I learned to tie scarves around my head, as I'd done at the age of eight, from memory and without ever having tried before, one day when I dressed up as an African for a school party. I wore a little doll on my back and a brownish camisole. What a genius opportunity, a person disguising herself as what she already is, at once distancing and duplicating herself. Was it I who said that one day in my life Carnaval came to an end? This was perhaps the only mask that could reveal me, exposing the distance that separates me from what I am as an auspicious and not irretrievable idea. It was not history that separated us: it was becoming a person. I never actually became the African lady I went dressed as that day, but one day I will become an African lady. Years later, fleeting moments come to mind when I learned something important while watching the women in my life get dressed and do their makeup, or while scrutinizing their personal belongings.

I would like to fixate on this bemusement, lying belly-down on the bed as they get ready in front of the mirror, the bedroom air overtaken by their perfume, for which I am, even now, still not of age. I observe their mix of skillfulness and haste, my silent by-and-by, the suspension of time, the low hum of concentration. It is at these moments, when we discover in others the perfection of habit, that we discover our nature as contemplative animals. Later, seizing an opening after they've taken off, I spend the afternoon dressing myself up in front of the same mirror. I try on their clothing; with no one to see me, I talk to myself, I hum a tune while reading the advice column in *Maria*, washing my face soon after and then reapplying the makeup in an awkward configuration. The pleasure, then, is found in the action and not the effect. I forget about the smudges on my face the entire afternoon, and they catch me not because their lipsticks are squashed and out of place, but because my face is still dirty when the adults arrive. This solitude is the beginning of becoming an individual.

Among these images, one sticks out: of a striking young woman whom my father would wed on what was, for me, the happiest day of the '90s. The bride danced in a miniskirt; she let herself be photographed drinking a coffee in a barren lot with the nonchalance and composure of a star: she knew she was beautiful and that we thought so. For fifteen years, the smashed-up lipsticks belonged to her. According to this theory of aesthetics, where beauty and independence are mutually dependent, my Portuguese mother, the eye behind nearly all of the photographs in this childhood album, played the role of curator of the independence necessary to make me a person and, finally, the patience at my hesitation to allow my picture to be taken, since eclipsed. To think that her perfume—carried by the afternoon breeze, reaching me at the kitchen table as I told her of my schoolyard exploits, she listening with the devotion of a blood sister—is the scent that these pages have forgotten, as though they were written on a scented notepad locked away for years in a drawer. Without a photographer, there is no album, and even when neither exists, what we still know of childhood are the eyes that looked to us, gazed at us, endured us, loved us.

Visiting salons has been a way of visiting different countries and learning to distinguish the features and manners of each, giving new fuel to prejudices. Senegal is a pair of moisturized hands; Angola a certain casualness, a brutal grace; Zaire a disaster; Portugal a burn from a hair dryer, the flesh wound left by a brush. I remember Tina, from Guinea-Conakry, a girl who did my hair in Mercês and shared a similar distrust of the Portuguese; but I can color in this map with the angel from another day, Lena, the Angolan girl who saved me one afternoon. I walked into a shopping-center hair salon; the woman turned to me before I could get a word out, skipping me to the front of the line; she washed my head with inexplicable care; she dunked a towel in hot water four times to soften my hair and then dried it, offering advice—"In my family we also have all sorts of mixes"—with a pride that is the primary motive for this book. I asked her name. She asked mine. She cut my tips, I left. I returned twice to look for Lena. The other day, I surprised her at the end of her shift; she was majestic, doing her own hair and short on time. I asked for the most common of my various hairstyles, which would take two hours—it was raining when I left.

In Portugal, Tina had gotten her start by braiding clients' hair at home, where I once visited her, but she had managed to invest in a salon that I visited in its very first (its last?) days, a similarly crammed space where she gave me a photo album to peruse, a compilation of her best work throughout the years, yellowed photographs, taken at an angle and out of focus, featuring women who'd just had their hair done, their look of pride, dresses faded in spots from Fanta can stains and fingerfuls of relaxer. The album is the antithesis of my own disheveled albums, and, at the same time, it describes the arc of my hair's drama, showing day one, the best day of each woman's hair. In a halting Portuguese, she had asked me days earlier on the telephone how I wanted to do my hair, and then I had run to the pharmacy on São Domingos, next to the Praça da Figueira, where a team of your typical Portuguese pharmacy workers doled out advice to old ladies and African girls from the outskirts of Lisbon about the best products, as though they were true specialists on these women's hair. The pharmacy looks on to a store selling seeds and fertilizers, and a bakeshop where one can buy banana bread, manioc, and smoked catfish, Queijo de Azeitão and port wine.

The fine men of São Domingos offer beauty tips, say, "Girl, this is just what your hair needs, this is just the thing, don't think twice." How to do justice to these Good Samaritans, who time after time came through for me, who heap praise on the hair of the cleaning ladies, make a pittance, and yet still call them "pretty lady": the six o'clock ladies on the streetcar, the subway, the "boat to Cacilhas," the bus, women I never meet in the hallway, with their hair glued to their head, in a pigtail, the color uneven, other times sparse, invisible to the occupant one seat back; wearing turtlenecks beneath polar ice jackets, the children abandoned to the public schools, for whom winter means the double torture of floor cleaner and acrylic wax, urine spots, hairs on the toilet seat; transported in minibuses by other women and scattered throughout public buildings where they take out the trash, wipe down toilet seats, throw out half-consumed bottles of water, and shuffle the papers they dust, wash coffee cups that I find lined up all in a row, breathe in their share of asbestos, perhaps sit at my desk and scribble their names on a sheet of paper, or furtively bang out letters on the keyboard like typist girls getting ready in front of our mirror before heading out to initial forms posted behind bathroom doors? If only I were capable of rising to the level of the gentlemen of São Domingos who address plain women as "pretty lady," an automatic and sales-pitchy "pretty lady" that, over before it's begun, may never reach their ears. It is the status of a proper pharmacy counter "pretty lady" to which these pages aspire, a celebration of words that, when said, are quickly ignored by he who says them, by she who hears them, a figure of speech, a waste of time, a mere formality.

12

In another photograph, the hair at my wedding. This was the handiwork of Roberto, a Brazilian hairdresser who had come to my aid after the lilac-haired girl at the reception desk informed me that they didn't work with hair like mine. I called Roberto, who gave me a business card, scheduling a three-hour appointment for the day of the wedding. He would arrive an hour late, sleepy and complaining about his boss, at the Pombaline-style apartment where he did my hair, a salon on the Avenida da Liberdade. An hour later, we both realized we wouldn't have enough time. I can still see my asymmetric hair, its volume on the left side greater than the right; I'd asked him to make it a classic. How I missed Dona Mena that day, wielding my hair into an event. At night, many miles from there, I undid the already inscrutable style with some help, recovering my long hair. It would have been better to give in to Tina's album and risk painting it blonde, a fashion that would last a month, a honeymoon with style. But what do I know? The salon on the Avenida had been the first following my financial emancipation, after a short-lived fidelity to a hairdresser in the Graça district who was fine with performing a brushing after I applied relaxer myself at home, letting it run down my body, the bathtub, the product full of toxicity, waiting for the foam to change colors as the instructions commanded, terrified by the warning about the risk of blindness. The painful lineage of my wedding-day coif, which for Mila and Roberto lasted no longer than the space of a yawn, would find in this neighborhood salon, a mere fifteen hundred feet from Sapadores, a chance convalescence. The lady in Graça threaded hair for the lion's share of her clients, and the last time I saw her, on my way to another neighborhood, she begged me not to stop taking care of myself. The salon in Graça dates back to the time when I felt no yearning for Luanda. As difficult as it was for me then to speak for myself in the middle of getting my hair washed, I ask myself today how I can give voice to the owner of that salon who, with infinite generosity and patience, buoyed the daily lives of the aged neighbors in an aesthetic disaster that would have infuriated my Grandpa Manuel; how, I ask myself, can I speak for another. If the Other is a wrinkle, emerging

only in the attempt to hit upon the necessary persever-
ance to remember that Other, how then to dare to be her
spokesperson? I would need a spokesperson for myself, a
language for what I see as the unbridgeable gap between
the easy answers and thoughtful answers, between the
hairdresser in Graça and my departure for another obscure
neighborhood, another salon, the gap between me and the
person I was becoming along the way; a language that,
impermeable to all subterfuge, was capable of escaping this
stormy journey without further setbacks, other than that of
my own state of mind.

It costs me great effort to picture once again, at the far
corner of the salon in Graça, the cubicle belonging to the
beautician who had settled there of her own accord. It was
no larger than a pantry. She had decorated it with a doll-
house, a little circle of *degradé* bottles of nail polish whose
rosy tones matched that of the two fish in her aquarium.
On cardboard shelves, she displayed pinchbeck necklaces
and bracelets purchased at the market in Martim Moniz,
which she resold to the old ladies in the neighborhood
whose toenails she adorned with flowers and cornucopias,
preserved for posterity with cell phone photos, a color-
ful collection of self-portraits, not handicrafts. Among
the hairdressers at the salon in Graça, similarly wanting
in resources, there was not a soul with less of an air of
someone merely passing through, though in fact she was
passing through on her way to Penha de França, where

she dreamed of opening her own place. That dream, which would become reality a few months later, was part of the dignity that leaves the lightest of imprints each time we register a memory. It isn't the hand of the writer that stands between him and God while he writes: it's who we believe ourselves to be that intrudes on a lifetime of trips to the salon, bringing us to believe that God is not to be found in some salon cubicle, that we must seek Him out in depths worthy of His presence. It occurs to me that I never shared what I did for a living with any of my hairdressers. I never made the effort to explain my occupation to them, as though they were incapable of understanding. While they did my hair, I spoke little of myself, as the years stretched on, less for a lack of patience than for a bashfulness inflamed by the all-too-human atmosphere of the salons. This reserve, which today I look back on with certain shame, led me involuntarily to moments when, appearing to flee from myself, I found the personal dignity preserved by a changing cast of hairdressers more befitting, robbing myself of the chance to have some part in what was just women's talk, wearing the same evasive expression my Grandpa Manuel had on those mornings when I returned from the hairdresser with my Grandma Lúcia. It's something of a surprise to me, then, that this tale of my trips to the salon over the years describes my experiences via a truce with myself, a privilege we can attain only in the company of others. In retrospect, I regret having surmised such a thing to be a shift away from my life, as though conflating this truce with the result of complex acrobatics that I could attain only through concentration. It was here all this time, not in this loose-leaf remembrance, but in the path of this hair that I tended to conflate with a wholly personal quest. It was there with me on every bus I ever took, if I'd only had the nobility of character to, as I shared with a Marine veteran the story of every Lisbon *mulata*, share a little less of my own story. This is my aim each time I evoke the beautician in Graça, who never laid a finger on my hair, though memory's complacency only casts me straight into paranoia, toxic baths, implacability, somnambulism, and complaints about the random choice of nameless men and women to whom I entrusted my hair throughout the years. This complacency is the path to a form of fraudulence, that of making us the lead actors in our lives, diminishing those in secondary roles. All memory is a mystery, I realize, only to be surprised by the revelation that we remember nothing of ourselves except in the company of others. In the Portugal that I was bequeathed, it was only in the salons, anticipating the frustration to be induced by the hairstyles at my side, that I allowed myself to rest, which shows me that it was in the salons, above all, during this undervalued truce with myself, that I was truly Portuguese.

I realize that I've been putting off shaving my head, as I've insisted on doing for three years during which I have visited not a single salon. This hairstyle belongs to what can be said, though perhaps it coincides with what we cannot say, as well. During those years, when I was often compared to Ronaldinho, who, entirely by chance, I later rediscovered retired and obese, I also stopped thinking about my hair. All the same, it would not be the oblivion of my youth, of the headscarf, of puberty, but a total oblivion: armistice. My exuberance, which my Grandpa Manuel always spoke of with pride, causing me to blush—the midnight extensions in São Gens; scaling the tower speakers at Saturday's, which I climbed with the help of strangers, never looking down; another time on a quarter pony—would get lost along the way. The hair and the writing would one day need to come together like a couple after a long separation. The book of my hair, meanwhile, would demand the effort of leaving literature waiting at the door, as my husband has waited for me outside salons throughout the years in four different cars, calling me to ask if I've already finished, worried he'll be spotted by the girls at the salons, so often filled with prejudice, remaining in the car to spare me the commentary, listening to the radio, checking messages on his phone, passing the time. In this book of my hair, it's literature that passes the time in the car and looks back at me without at first recognizing me when I climb in and ask if he likes it.

My hair would wait for me at the beginning of the journey, in the morning-time image of the streets of Oeiras,

on the Cesário Verde Promenade where I would walk to
elementary school and where today I walk as though a
trauma were not a physical presence. It is for this reason
that I say that this book was composed methodically, re-
capitulating the only story that I feel in the right to tell,
the story, known to some, of the looks African women
exchange when they cross on Lisbon streets, studying one
another's hairdos, clothes, boyfriends—and, every now
and then, exchanging smiles. As do the little girls being
dragged along by mothers weighed down by shopping
bags. I was once this girl, in a café my dad brought me
to at the age of seven and where I would spend several
hours observing a young biracial woman who, I thought,
I might one day resemble. She wore a red blouse and was
speaking to a table of friends beneath my attentive gaze,
the adults intervening to close my mouth each time my
jaw dropped. I thought that one day I would be like her,
so naturally I stared at her hair, thinking that childhood
was a temporary phase from which someone would come
to save me. That is why, to this day, I wave to the girls who
see in me the girl they will one day be and who are the
best judges, girls who don't pronounce "how is that" the
same way their mothers do, girls who share my prosody,
and perhaps already know their hair better than I know
mine. I wave to them and smile down from the grown-up
world, their own future revealed—and continue on my
way. I see again the looks directed my way on the street

and the occasional "good morning" that we don't hold back, me and my African sisters, thinking, I can take care of that hair for you, I'll show you how it's done. Aunties offer me kerchiefs in the most lively colors: "Mila, this one goes great with your skin tone." "I know, you're right, you're right." "You have to find a style of your own: you had one before." I persist in seeking everything in neutral tones, transformed into the idea I have of myself, though I find all sorts of adjectives to describe them, as though I had all the time in the world. Perhaps this isn't what it is to yearn for something, perhaps this isn't the name for having embodied the answer to a psychodrama that I pretend makes me feel like laughing.

13

I never took care of my hair the way I did during the autumn when Mila lost her mind. I also didn't learn anything at all during these months spent sleeping, or else in front of the mirror undertaking a deranged toilette, eating toothpaste behind the bathroom door, listening to the helicopters land on the other side. Belonging to a large family can distract us from our predictable woes. It's no use waiting for genetics to rear its head. I had dealt with this possibility with the reserve of new parents poking fun at the overeagerness of family members to discover some resemblance in their newborns. My own madness would appear at the moment when I finally came to the conclusion that I didn't look like anyone. We never have such a strong resemblance to others as when we believe ourselves to be independent. The blow, then, resides in shedding light on the way that our life began before our inception, a finding we can live only passively.

I'd had my inception a century earlier, drooling all over a pillowcase in which I thought I recognized alleyways from my neighborhood, familiar features, clapping my hands for no good reason or preoccupied with a change in the light, like some great-great-grandmother in an insane asylum in Porto. What followed would not, however, be an opportunity to get to know myself but an occasion that would bring an end to my faith in the possibility of coming to know myself on my own. There isn't much to learn from the lion's share of things that happen to us, despite what we hear said about how everything makes us better people. Much less is there anything that we can learn alone, though we exalt lone wolves and their solitary callings, which nonetheless cannot conceal the pouty lips they got from their grandparents, or the noble self-reproach inherited from their mothers.

It's often said that everything happens for a reason, but this is nothing more than a way for human horror to grapple with injustice. There's a pettiness in our needing to learn that justice does not exist, pettiness in the sense of being proportional to our minority position vis-à-vis the grandiose scale of the world around us. If injustice results from the lack of meaning in the events that happen to us and that we have trouble accepting, it also offers the possibility of staking a claim to a certain share of grace in our lives. For this reason, redemption resides not in our finding a meaning for everything but in the possibility of wonder in the face of the grace to be found in the arbitrary. And yet the path is not open to us to seek it.

During the months I believed I was a vampire or Joan of Arc, finding rhyme and reason in everything, impeccably coiffed and made up to visit the doctor and scrawling out plans on napkins at the table of a neighborhood tavern, an auspicious parapet, fifteenth-century battle plans to face the apathy of regular customers whose eyes were glued to the *Correio da Manhã* all the while thinking we were actually in the fifteenth century, neither made me a better person nor brought me closer to discovering who I am. Losing my mind represented the possibility of reclaiming my nationality, though it didn't spare me the irony of there being little in my mode of suffering that set me apart. Autumn marched on for the old folks at the tavern, with day after day of sporting championships and violent crimes; it marched on at home, too, with chores, meals, finances, and the election of Barack Obama. I was stuck in the past. "You don't know yourself," I repeat today as though convinced, to only later hit up against my curiosity about myself with each step I take. I was not the wonder that I had anticipated but the question that I set in my path. I watched my disincarnate heart pass by atop a crude reliquary fashioned from crepe paper and wood glue on a quiet Sunday morning in the neighborhood. The year's work of a scouting troop: a peculiar sculpture brought before the public for a few brief, if anxiously awaited, moments, and later stuffed into a damp basement. "Why do people hang blankets from the windows?" a child who watched a procession with me once asked. "Because it's tradition," I replied. "What's *that*?" the child asked. I didn't notice that I could not run from confronting who I am—even if who I am is something I can see only from a far and misleading distance. I learned not to fear plunging deep into myself, an experience that can feel like a personal victory. That autumn interlude led me back to the time when *I* once again became a letter learned from a school primer, something we never stop being, even if we become experts in speaking on our own behalf. I say "I," "I myself," but mastering the ability to say it is like going back to being a letter on a school chalkboard, an ability I'd neglected. This "I" comes to us at the moment we recognize on the written page things we already knew how to express. It is a playground where I am allowed to try out not only new words but expressions learned long ago.

I repeat "I," "I myself," trying to find myself around the house on a dark night. At this moment, I am an ancient old hunchback seated at the hearth next to the fire, back in Seia before my Portuguese family made for Mozambique halfway into the fifth decade of the twentieth century. This old woman would spend the night nodding off in front of the fire, seated imperceptibly in an armchair and seeping into the darkness from which she emerged to call after the children of the house, who lived in fear of her. This was in the time when they still couldn't find their way alone through the dark. They were unfamiliar with the angle of the furniture and not yet able to pick out the shadows, which they didn't connect with the objects as seen in the light of day. The hunched old woman would call to them, "Come here," in her faded voice, sitting them on her lap, pulling them close and then shaking them until in the distance the sound of tiny footsteps could be heard. Then she'd ship the little ones off from her lap, saying, "Get, get, get," as though she feared they would carry her off, and then she returned to the same position, settling back with her faraway gaze into the chair, becoming the chair, leaving the little ones to make sense of this change in disposition. I note in her the calling of the past urging me to come closer to give me a thwack, offering me a glass of warm milk, ears attuned to the activity in the hallway and attention divided.

The people we were one day do not always call to us with such conviction but rather, at times, exhibit the bashfulness of estranged family members listening in on our conversations, waiting for the right moment to engage us. This past is not independent of me when I rouse my shadow and come to the kitchen to look for the old woman who I thought was looking for me. Watching as the reliquary passed by was to learn to walk in the dark, to trust in the stranger at home who, after all, was only me, the two of us thinking that we had been carrying on this romance because we had been waiting for one another, seeking an opening in the adults' attention. The old woman sitting in front of the chimney in Seia thought it was she who summoned the children and was lord over her tender little thwacks, when it was the children who had gone looking for her, understanding, without knowing how to explain it, the elusive nature of her affection and in fact having no fear of her at all, but rather the sort of curiosity one has for a salamander or a stove: a curiosity similar to the old lady's for the touch of a tiny nose or the children's sweaty necks at nighttime. When we reach each other without having sought each other out, we come face-to-face with our share of grace.

"Where did I leave Mila?" I ask myself, as though looking for the house keys. Will I have stayed behind in Beira, in '77, reading a newspaper out loud in the shadow of a papaya tree, or will I be that paint smudge on the photograph of a dam, also in Mozambique? Will I be the water stains on my Grandpa Manuel's desk; a pen in Grandpa Castro's suitcase; a flea in the mattress in São Gens? Finding someone may be a sign that we had been looking for them. Still, it seems to me that "finding" isn't a given result of "looking" when we're speaking of people.

Finding myself is closer to finding a flea while looking for a blot of paint; finding a water stain when we were looking for a key; finding a pen when we were looking for a person. What is found reconfigures what was sought. The search for an origin and an identity doesn't reconstitute my origin or uncover my identity. A person finds herself only by chance.

"Where did I leave Mila?" The time spent searching coincides with the time spent discovering, exactly as if I realized the purpose of what I write in the course of writing it. The person I found by chance is intertwined with the result of my search only in the sense that, if we use a shovel to unearth a chest, the shovel will sometimes leave a mark on the chest. Such a conclusion shows me that this is my hair only by chance. Who we become in writing is as different from who we are as a water stain is different from a key.

What would my street look like on a winter morning, on the way to school, seen by a pigeon perched atop a lamppost? The pigeon may see me, observing my reflection in the rare vitrine along the Cesário Verde Promenade I took each morning. I would think about how I looked in a new pair of shoes given me by Grandma Lúcia, one size too big. The pigeon would launch some excrement my way, which would fragment in the air. On that cold, dark path where you couldn't find a living soul, we were, the pigeon and I, the only discernible forms of life: I, completely self-absorbed, learning about solitude in solitude—seeking life within; the pigeon trembling with cold to the beat of its tiny heart, a negation of the mind: a heart with feathers. Perhaps we didn't even notice one another. Above the pigeon, rain falls on certain mornings, without our being able to determine its origin. An origin has no desire to know where it originates—it doesn't know what an origin is. Starting from this abstract point, my hair is mere movement, a sign of life that in no way sets itself apart from the other bodies caught in the rain. The Oeiras of my childhood and the inner realm of its inhabitants are, for the rain, not so much a place as an arbitrary destination. This indifference that characterizes nature, to which we are the only exceptions, pains me each time I see how far my mind has come, the only redeeming aspect of my hair's vagaries, its successive cuts and neglect a futile reminder. I'm assailed by the shock and the despair that at times distress me, walking today along the street, in the face of the evidence that each person whose path I cross carries a life within them. So many, so many, so many people, *so much* life, I think before retreating into myself.

I play no part in the pigeon's life. I am merely a living body passing by. The person I might have been is not the caricature I yearn for. It is a person. That person would say: "So many, so many, so many people, *so much* life." I might, perched atop my lookout, or even in the midst of a crowd, contemplate my origin, and in bearing witness to it find myself as lost for words as the pigeon watching me on the way to school. From my lookout, I am perhaps a harebrained observer of my mind's expansion. I could not observe my passage while in motion myself. The rain, meanwhile, wants nothing to do with us—it doesn't choose its fools—and is, seen from a distance, a tiny thing.

14

My father once covered the distance between Beira and Luanda atop a scooter. This was at the end of the '70s, at the time when his parents had moved from Mozambique to Angola, where my grandfather was to begin a new job after a decade and a half of building dams. That journey and the choice to make it by scooter represent in my imagination the pure elation of my father's independence at a time when he was still an adolescent. He had refused to make the trip by plane and had gone by scooter, as though he were covering a distance of two city blocks.

Beyond this, everything that I see and hear is an endless stretch of desert interrupted by the hum of a scooter. This is absurd, I'm well aware, and geographically puerile. Still, I like to think of him crossing the desert, the savanna, the mountains, the rivers, and the villages, kicking up red, copper, magenta dust, without ever getting stuck, to the irritating background noise of the motor that, as it passes, trails off like a brief synopsis of anyone's youth. I think about this trip as the opposite of clerical wanderings through the desert, made in silence yet speaking equal volumes.

One day after crossing into Angola, my father found himself before a *Welwitschia mirabilis*, a desert species particular to that spot, renowned for its uselessness. The *Welwitschia* can survive for centuries off limited resources and serves no particular purpose, whether for zebras or for human beings. This species is one of creation's wastes of energy, as we might remark annoyedly about flies. Placed in my father's path, this plant was like so many other things in the natural world: an obstacle that reveals the purpose behind our insistence. That doesn't mean that the plant's lack of purpose was a clue to some absurd plan to cross the continent on a scooter, traversing the rose-colored map. It was, however, a greater sign of the call of meaninglessness that hovers over everything we do. My father had no reason to think he was the first man to catch sight of the ugly plant: he didn't hail the sight with a buck of his front wheel; he didn't stop his scooter.

I don't know what he might have stuffed into the backpack that I see across his shoulders. Before me, I have remnants of Mozambique. Grandpa Manuel's desk, which belonged to my father; four photographs of water gushing forth from a dam my grandfather had designed; a photograph of him and his colleagues from the hydroelectric utility where he worked in Beira; an English translation of the Bible, perhaps used by my Grandma Lúcia to read an afternoon psalm following a round of canasta. In a video, Grandpa Manuel, barely past forty, scrawls *1967* across some sandy beach, the year that can also be glimpsed on the front page of a newspaper Grandma Lúcia peruses behind him. I don't know how to lead into the story of my hair, which appears to me like a dictionary entry whose corresponding meaning I can't identify. I cannot assume the place of my father's backpack, nor my own.

15

The one time I got my hair done with a woman from London who was trying her luck in the Chiado, it was plain to see the salon would not last long. For an hour and a half, she destroyed all my previous hairdressers, who, she claimed, had ruined my hair. "It's been a year since my last haircut," I said to her out of habit. She straightened my hair with hot combs, which she carefully removed from a toaster oven, a modern version of the combs I'd seen heated over coal in the markets of Luanda and used to scare me. After an interval of three months, I returned only to find chains on the door: to be expected.

I think that what I've always sought, beyond trying to learn to stand up to hairdressers and their bullying, was to live a story of fidelity. A friend once told me that her lifelong hairdresser had lost her touch. I thought that this was what I wanted, a hand I could entrust myself to and that might show me the way: a guiding hand. The story of these tribulations, with its ups and downs, which return to me in a quiet and orderly stream, goes far beyond my own story and does not, strictly speaking, belong to any one individual. It is the story of shuttered businesses, of unmet expectations and changes of plans, of telephones, of jobs, of houses, of those who leave their countries in search of a better life, a condition that immediately transforms anyone into someone who cannot be trusted, who doesn't pick up, come back soon, closed, who's moved, someone in transit, showing that we, too, are in constant motion. I look back at what's at risk of getting lost. My trips to the Almirante Reis in search of the famed Look Obama salon, the kind soul who complimented my hair the day I cut it for the last time, mourning its loss and worrying that I had lost my head. I see now that the tempo of this book ought to be punctuated not by haircuts and hairdos but by the time between each of these. I sought fidelity, seeing myself as a fixed point by which to measure the transience of the ladies at each salon. I never went anywhere: I've stayed put.

Crossing Almirante Reis by car, looking for the number of a store that's now shuttered, another negative salon, a solution, I was looking for myself without realizing that the frustration preceding my search was the necessary condition for this story I was seeking subject matter for, in the belief that I lacked material for my book. I take comfort in noticing that I preempted this biography with the same haste that causes me to confuse growing pains with chronic ones. For the good of my provisional capillary woes, and thanks to a happy revisionism, I give in to the thought that I've closed a chapter, possibly that of my hair's childhood. I've lived a novel, without realizing that what I write now is the leftover scraps of that book. I try as I might to remember that I'm still alive and that my vision of things suffers from a deceptive proximity. My writing is a prosthetic limb kept in reserve for the arms I'll lose along the way. I read over the list of salons, I refuse to find meaning: my way of silencing the adverse effects, the very real risk described on the packaging, the itching, the burning, my latent condition of amputee, the recurring word *abrasive*, literarily respectable, the soft politics of the search for sun and water by the young kids who take fatal leaps at the edge of the sea, kids we always feared for, at a time when every adventure ended with a quadriplegic. The elliptical narrative of the unfinished biography of my hair, to which the brittleness of memory compels me, frustrates any philosophy of hair. That would require an elephant's memory, not a rebellious lion's mane. How could I hope to make a politics from this private drama?

16

The only time I crossed Lisbon in search of an ornament for my hair, I was after a silk magnolia as a finishing touch for my wedding day. On the Rua da Conceição, in a milliner's shop, I was persuaded of the singularity of a rhinestone tiara, which I would end up using during the ceremony. It was not, however, the search for and selection of the tiara, nor its debut on my wedding day, that made it what it is today. On the day of the wedding, it turned out to be a bad purchase, slipping from my straightened hair. When I got home, I left it in a drawer. Years later, I found a display case for it. I'd filled the display case with knickknacks and photographs, and then I remembered the tiara. At that moment it became clear to me, as I arranged it in its new home, that the display case was meant for the tiara, and that the tiara was not fit to be used but to be shown.

I see it each day as I pass through the hallway. It doesn't remind me of the day I used it. There inside its case, it is an emblem of this whole hairy drama. I hold on to it like some antique, as if I'd married fifty years ago, or as if I had inherited it. I don't remember, it's true, it ever having been mine, as though a trip to the store could provide the opportunity to forge my ancestry, to come across a family relic that I hadn't realized was missing. It calls out to me—"Mila, I presume"—initiating a conversation I can't quite make out. It's also a reminder that it's when things are laid bare that we begin to perish.

My truncated notion of the person I never became is the same as that Maria da Luz had of Lisbon, the truncated concept of Conceiçao or Josefina preserved by her pathetic blurry portrait, the elliptical telegram I received from my parents' youth, the even more elliptical telegram of my anxieties and expectations at any age. Today, I see all this smoke as a face made blurry by the years, the caricature (I know I'm repeating myself) of the person who, having never come to be, I insist on repeating I will not become, as though I need to convince myself of it. Now, with the proper distance, I see that I was this double face, that I'm the one who disturbs it and tells it what to do, the one who marks the tempo of its whistling, the one who ridicules its flattened nose. Meanwhile, and I shudder at the thought, it is this mask that I yearn for, as though memory's mawkish tendencies betrayed the best intentions and restored my true self like a costume that makes me laugh and cry as though it were not degrading. It is memory, overwhelming me with shame at my inability to regard things with the fullness of grace, that leads me to this face. I fear then that if I myself apprehend it in this way, others might understand it as an adulteration, as though fraudulence were a property acquired by private memory the moment it becomes public (a spiritual sung quietly on the bus) and which, when it comes to my hair, tosses me into the slurry of collective memory, losing sight of the world as it appears from the display case: the accidents of the heart of the "good girl" that each one of us has the right to carry within her—accidents of anonymity. The trap of sentimentality suddenly becomes clear to me, the way I slip through my own fingers: the face I long to see again, the same one I do not recognize as my own, does not reveal me except to myself.

I cannot maintain my self-awareness at the same time as I call forth these memories, nor can I settle on a moral to these memories, which, left to their own devices, bring me back to who I am beneath the form of the duo who deserve both my disgust and my deference, leading me to disavow the mask only to realize a short time later that what truly deserves my disavowal is this inability to embrace that borrowed and impoverished concept of what I also am. What is the point of bringing Mila into the light only to confirm that bringing her out into the open is the dust kicked up by our passing caravan?

The tiara in the display case gives me back to myself as decoration for my hair. The hair is the person. The subterfuge of comedy, the aspiration to a peaceful drama, are the adornments. "Make a museum of yourself and reveal what could already be seen." The redundancy emerges when, beneath tissue paper, inside the box that we know contains something, the tiara is revealed. Writing is similar to taking a brush to a head of hair perched atop a Styrofoam bust. And if the hair is the person and I the tiara, if it is I who am mere decoration, if it was myself I locked up in the display case in the hopes of watching our cinema from a private box, who then is Mila?

DJAIMILIA PEREIRA DE ALMEIDA is the author of five books: the novels *That Hair, A visão das plantas,* and *Luanda, Lisboa, Paraíso,* as well as *Ajudar a cair,* a portrait of a community of people with cerebral palsy, and *Pintado com o pé,* a collection of essays. Her writing has appeared in *Blog da Companhia das Letras, Common Knowledge, Granta.com, Granta Portugal, Ler, Revista Pessoa, Quatro Cinco Um, Revista serrote, Words Without Borders, Revista ZUM,* and elsewhere.

ERIC M. B. BECKER is a translator and editor of *Words Without Borders.* He has translated work by numerous writers from the Portuguese, including Mia Couto, and has received fellowships and grants from the National Endowment for the Arts, the Fulbright Commission, and the PEN/Heim Translation Fund.